The Trouble
with Skye

◁∘∘ KEYSTONE STABLES ∘∘▷

BOOK 1

The Trouble with Skye

by
Marsha Hubler

Zonderkidz

Zonder**kidz**®

The children's group of Zondervan

www.zonderkidz.com

The Trouble with Skye
Copyright © 2004 by Marsha Hubler

Requests for information should be addressed to:
Grand Rapids, MI 49530

Library of Congress Cataloging-in-Publication Data

Hubler, Marsha, 1947–
    The trouble with Skye / Marsha Hubler.—1st ed.
        p. cm.— (Keystone Stables)
    Summary: Thirteen-year-old Skye, a troubled foster child, comes to
live at Keystone Stables, a Christian home where she discovers her love for
horses.
    ISBN 0-310-70572-X (softcover)
    [1. Horses—Fiction. 2. Foster home care—Fiction. 3. Christian life—
Fiction.] I. Title.
PZ7.H86325Tr 2004
[Fic]—dc22   2003018869

Special thanks to the Glupker family for use of their ranch.

Editor: Barbara J. Scott
Interior design: Susan Ambs
Interior illustrations: Lyn Boyer
Art direction: Laura Maitner
Cover design: Gayle Raymer
Photography: Synergy Photographic

Printed in the United States of America

04 05 06 07 08 09 /❖DC/ 10 9 8 7 6 5 4 3 2 1

This book is dedicated to all children and
horse lovers everywhere.

My deepest appreciation to my editor Barbara Scott,
whose expertise and kind advice were a constant
encouragement to write for God's glory.

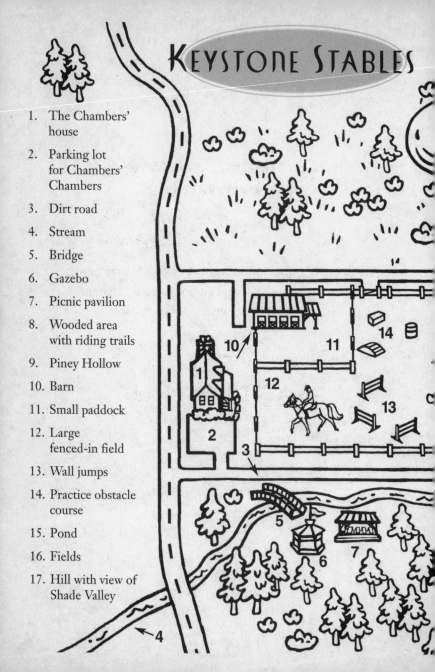

Keystone Stables

1. The Chambers' house
2. Parking lot for Chambers' Chambers
3. Dirt road
4. Stream
5. Bridge
6. Gazebo
7. Picnic pavilion
8. Wooded area with riding trails
9. Piney Hollow
10. Barn
11. Small paddock
12. Large fenced-in field
13. Wall jumps
14. Practice obstacle course
15. Pond
16. Fields
17. Hill with view of Shade Valley

Map of the Chambers' Ranch

Chapter One

Young lady, and I use that term loosely, I'm tired of your despicable behavior. You have exhausted this court's patience. I'm sending you to the Chesterfield Detention Center and throwing away the key!"

Skye Nicholson looked cold as an ice cube as she slumped in the wooden chair and stared back at Judge Mitchell. Most ordinary thirteen-year-olds would have been scared to death at a hearing with an angry judge yelling at the top of his lungs. But Skye was no "ordinary" thirteen-year-old. Her anger matched the judge's. Only Wilma Jones, her court-appointed lawyer, prevented Skye from exploding.

"Cool it," the lawyer squeezed out of her mouth as she grabbed Skye's arm.

Skye opened her mouth and yawned deliberately, pulling her arm from the woman's grasp. Her brown eyes pinched into slits as she shoved her fingers through her long dark hair. She folded her arms, then slumped down further, stretching her legs under the table and crossing them with a jolt. Her glare shifted from the judge to the anxious attorney seated next to her.

"Get real," Skye snapped. Her lips tightened into an unmistakable display of disgust as she once again turned her scowling face to the judge.

"Twenty years on the bench in Pennsylvania, and I have never seen a record like this for a girl your age," the judge continued. He slid reading glasses onto his face and lifted a paper. "Five foster homes. Drug and alcohol abuse, vandalism, shoplifting—and that's just this past year! This reads like a record for someone at the state pen!" Continuing down the paper, he pointed sharply at the bottom. "Oh—and this is the best part. You didn't do any of it! C'mon, Skye," the judge barked as he yanked off his glasses and glared, "what do you think I am, stupid?"

Skye popped into an upright position, mouth open, more than willing to answer. "Now that you ask—" she sassed.

Wilma glared and dug five long red fingernails into Skye's arm. "Knock it off!" she whispered.

Skye wasn't one to take advice from anyone, even if polished nails were sinking into her flesh. With a yank, she pulled free and folded her arms. Then, down she went into her super slump, staring at a scratch in the table. She glanced up at the judge, and then looked down again.

"It's not a question of *if* you are going, but for how long!" Judge Mitchell declared.

The paneled courtroom, damp and empty except for six people, held an eerie quiet. All that could be heard was April's rain pelting the towering windows on each side. Nothing stirred for what seemed like hours.

Skye glanced at the judge and then at the plump court reporter sitting in front of his bench. Everyone was waiting. Skye leaned forward, resting her right elbow on the table. Placing her forehead on her open hand, she glanced to the left, past her lawyer who sat with hands folded, to a man in a blue suit. *"Dork" Dansing, prosecuting attorney,* Skye thought, scowling. *He's always sticking his nose in my business.* Next to Dansing, pushed back from his table, sat a woman whom Skye had never seen before. Just as Skye's glance found her, the woman looked over and smiled.

Skye was so amazed that someone would actually smile at her that she couldn't help but stare. As silence radiated from the bench, Skye examined the new but interesting enemy.

Not bad for thirty-something, Skye thought.

The solid-framed woman wore a dark green pants suit. Two very blue eyes radiated from a pleasant face framed by short, frosted hair.

She looks like Ida Markham, Skye thought, remembering one of her former foster mothers. *Wonder if they're related? Could've come from the same litter.*

"Skye!" Wilma whispered. "The judge is waiting for some kind of response from you. Act like you're the least bit sorry and he might go easy. I'm trying to get your sentence shortened."

"Yeah, right," Skye returned in a loud sarcastic whisper.

"Girl, I'm trying to help you. Now cool it!"

Wilma stood. "Your Honor," she apologized, "I beg the court's indulgence. I think Skye has learned her lesson this time. She really is sorry." The lawyer gently placed her hand on Skye's shoulder.

Faking a faucet that had sprung a leak, Skye's eyes glistened with moisture as she stared at the judge. She realized that turning on the tears was her last hope to avoid Chesterfield. Skye crumpled her face into an Oscar-winning pout, and tears flowed down her red cheeks.

Wilma reached into her pocket and handed Skye a wad of tissues. Skye dabbed her eyes and blew her nose. With her drenched puppy-dog eyes and quivering lips, she repositioned in the chair, folded her hands around the tissues, and smiled innocently at the judge.

"I'm not buying it!" Judge Mitchell announced. "I've been through this act before, and it's getting a little old. Save your tears for Chesterfield, Skye. They don't work anymore. Sorry, Wilma. Nice try." The judge stacked a pile of papers. "Does anyone have anything else to say?"

"If it please the court," Samuel Dansing said, standing, "Eileen Chambers would like to request that she and her husband, Tom, be granted custody of Skye Nicholson. I believe Your Honor is aware of the Chambers' fine record as foster parents."

"Eileen," Judge Mitchell said emphatically, "I was afraid that's why you were here. You *don't* want this kid.

Trust me. She ran the last two sets of foster parents out of the business."

Eileen Chambers glanced over at Skye and then stood to her feet. "Your Honor, we'd really like to give this a try. We've had troubled kids before and—"

"Not like this one, you haven't. I mean it. You're diving in way over your heads."

"It's worth a try, Your Honor. I think we can help her."

Judge Mitchell leaned back in his leather chair and stroked his beard. He glanced at Eileen, then at Skye.

Eileen waited patiently. Skye sat quietly with fake ribbons of liquid trickling down her face.

"I'll consider my decision. Until then, we're adjourned," Judge Mitchell said. He rose, gathered a thick pile of folders, and hastened off to a side room, slamming the door.

After a week in juvenile hall, Skye found herself seated in front of a battered wooden desk at some place called Maranatha Treatment Center. All she knew was that she *wasn't* going to Chesterfield and she *would be* going to another foster home. The thought didn't seem to bother her one way or the other. *More foster parents. Big deal*, she told herself. Her last set of foster parents had dropped her off at the Children and Youth Agency two weeks ago.

Easy come; easy go. Another day in the life of an unwanted nobody, she thought, looking around the empty room. *So what else is new?*

Down in her super slump, Skye folded her arms and crossed her legs, her eyes exploring every corner of the cramped office. The walls were a faded yellow that matched the worn-out carpet perfectly. She took a deep breath and wrinkled her nose. *Yuck! Smells like the boys' locker room at school!*

She scanned the two big windows on either side of the desk and decided they were probably last painted before she was born. The only bright spots in the whole place were colored posters spaced evenly on the walls, posters about God—and courage—and peace. Finally, out of boredom, Skye focused on a name plaque on the desk:

Eileen Chambers
Special Needs Therapist

Great! Skye complained to herself. *Someone else who thinks she can figure me out. The only special 'need' I have is to get outta here!*

Behind her a door opened and closed. Skye looked up to see Eileen Chambers approaching the desk. The woman settled gracefully into a rickety swivel chair, looked at Skye, and smiled. Skye stared openly at her bright yellow T-shirt with the letters "MARANATHA" in rainbow colors splashed across the front.

"Good morning, Skye," Mrs. Chambers said. "How are you today?"

Skye lowered her head, her face wrinkling into a pout.

"Oh, the silent treatment?" the woman said. "Okay, have it your way—for now."

Skye listened while Mrs. Chambers shuffled papers, opened and shut drawers, and squeaked the stubborn chair. Finally, after what seemed like forever, the woman spoke, and Skye glanced up.

"According to this, you've got some pretty big problems," Mrs. Chambers said, holding up a folder with papers sticking out. She dropped it in the middle of the desk. "All of us here at Maranatha Treatment Center are willing and able to help you find some solutions, young lady."

Why does everybody who sits behind a desk call me "young lady"? Skye griped to herself. *They all know I'm not a young lady. Never have been—never will be.*

Mrs. Chambers leaned back in the chair as far as she could. "Skye, Judge Mitchell has placed you into our after-school program."

Skye just stared into her blue eyes.

"You certainly have made quite a reputation for yourself at Madison Middle School." The woman slipped a paper from the folder and placed it on the desk. "This list of offenses is something else. And what's with this assault on Hannah Gilbert? You threw soda in her face and set fire to her books."

"I just don't like her stupid face, that's all!" Skye snapped. "Some day I'm gonna punch her lights out."

"There's more to life than hating people. What are you trying to do? Prove you're the toughest kid at Madison?" Mrs. Chambers smiled discreetly.

"Yeah, that's it," Skye sneered.

"Anyway," the woman continued, "your life is about to take an about-face. Honey, you have so much potential, but it's buried pretty deep. We can help you find the other you."

"Honey's for bees, and I ain't sweet! My name is Skye!" She pulled her arms tighter against her chest.

"All right, *Skye,*" Eileen Chambers said sternly. "You have much to learn. One of those things is respect for authority." She leaned forward, folding her hands on top of a pile of folders. "Here's the deal. Are you listening?"

"Y-e-e-e-e-s-s-s!" Skye drew out her response like air escaping from a bicycle tire. She tightened her shoulders and clenched her fists.

"I hope you're willing to accept the terms of the judge's decision. Frankly, you have little choice. Your only other option is Chesterfield for who knows how long. I'm sure you'd rather not do that. Now, here's the plan." She pulled out another paper from the same folder. "First— and you're going to like this—you'll go back to Madison after you serve a ten-day suspension. You really should have been expelled, you know. But I think everyone is willing to give you one more chance since you'll be living with Mr. Chambers and me at Keystone Stables."

"What's Keystone Stables?" she grumbled.

Mrs. Chambers smiled again. "Well, it's our home for one thing. And it's also a special needs dude ranch, licensed by the State of Pennsylvania. We operate on state funding, grants, and private donations. You should love it there. But back to your daily routine, after school every day you will be transported by van here to Maranatha Treatment Center for counseling. Any questions so far?"

Skye folded her arms tighter. Staring at the floor, she counted slivers of caked mud left by other people's sneakers. Whether she was listening or not, this woman would never know.

"Look at me when I speak to you, young lady."

Silence. Finally, Skye felt compelled to look up.

"Thank you. Next, and most importantly, you will spend an unspecified length of time in our care, not only as a Maranatha client but also as a foster child in our home at Keystone. Maybe a year, maybe—it's all contingent on your behavior. The Johnsons have already brought all your clothes and signed the release papers, so we're ready to move you today. I'll be your caseworker here as well as your foster parent, so get ready. We're going to be spending a lot of time together—like it or not."

Skye snapped her head up. Her eyes flared, and her cheeks flushed with anger. "You have *got* to be kidding! You're going to be my counselor as well as my foster mother? I'd rather rot in juvie!" Skye angrily ran her fingers through her hair as she glared pitchforks at the woman.

"That can be arranged, Miss Nicholson!" the woman retorted as her blue eyes locked on Skye's. "We need to get some things straight right now!" She leaned forward way over her desk. "Sit up in that chair when I speak to you!"

Skye reluctantly sat up and scowled.

"Number one: your days of telling people what to do are over," Mrs. Chambers lectured.

"Number two: this is what the judge ordered. We will all comply with every word, including you."

"Number three: Chesterfield always has empty cells for kids who think they know everything. All I need to do is pick up that phone. Any questions?"

Eileen Chambers leaned back in her chair, certain she had made her point. "And one more thing: you may call me Mrs. Chambers or Mrs. C., but never Eileen. Is that clear?"

"Ei—I—I—" Skye's face turned red and ice hung from her voice.

"Yes, Miss Nicholson?" Mrs. Chambers said as she leaned forward, double daring Skye to try it.

"Ei—, I—, will I have my own bedroom?" Skye's voice changed, now showing some concern amidst her anger.

"It's all taken care of." Mrs. Chambers relaxed. "We have lots of room at our house. And," she added with a twinkle in her eye, "there's also a surprise waiting for you."

Chapter Two

Welcome to Keystone Stables, Skye!" Mrs. Chambers said as they climbed out of the van. Skye followed Mrs. Chambers up a long ramp onto the porch of a ranch home in the country. The spring rains had given way to a warm breeze and a crystal-clear sky. Skye took a deep breath, trying to hide her feelings as she recalled the last few weeks.

Another foster home was nothing new for Skye Nicholson. As long as she could remember, she had lived in foster homes, but each one deepened her anger.

Her real parents? She wasn't sure. All she knew was that when she was three, there had been a car accident, and she had been taken to live with strangers. As she grew older, Skye asked Child Protective Services about her parents. They would only tell her that she had been placed in foster care because her parents were involved with drugs.

But where are my parents? Are they even alive? If they are, don't they want me?

Those questions haunted Skye at night and now they ate away at her stomach as she faced more strangers with more rules that she had no intention of obeying.

Mrs. Chambers, juggling a briefcase and groceries, struggled to find her house key but finally gave up and rang the doorbell. "I know someone's home," she said. "We'll just wait a few moments."

"What do you think I'm going to do? Run away?" Skye spouted as Mrs. Chambers rang the doorbell again.

Running away sounded better the more Skye thought about it, and it certainly wouldn't be the first time. She pictured the pavilion at the city park, her favorite hiding place behind the dumpster. It sure looked good right now. To be away from everything! Here she was again, doing what she hated the most, moving in with strangers.

What kind of a mess am I in this time? Skye thought as she scanned the front porch. The house was beige. Windows on each side of the door had blue shutters with carved hearts. A shiny brass knocker hung on the white front door. The cement floor wrapped around to her right, encased in fancy white railings and posts. Skye hated to admit, even though it was one more rotten foster home, this one had a homey feel to it. Just as she turned toward the yard, the door opened.

"Hi," a voice said.

Skye slowly turned.

"Come in," said a slender girl a few years older than Skye. The teenager had long, kinky red hair and tons of freckles that clashed with her bright red plaid shirt. She was sitting in a wheelchair!

One of Skye's favorite pastimes was keeping her outside from finding out what her inside was feeling. Inside, her mouth hung open; on the outside? A classic pout. *This is the surprise?* she fumed. *Just perfect. Another brat to make my life more miserable. And a crippled one at that. Now I know why I was brought here. Maid service!*

"I'm Morgan Hendricks." The girl tugged at a joystick on the right arm of her wheelchair, setting it in reverse. She extended her other hand in welcome.

Ignoring Morgan, Skye followed Mrs. Chambers into a spacious living room with country furniture and decorations that made it look like a craft shop. Peach walls surrounded a blue carpet, and the room smelled like cinnamon. Soft music played in the background.

In spite of herself, Skye liked the place just a little even though she didn't see a television—in that room at least. Everything felt warm, friendly, and different from any other foster home. Peaceful even.

"Welcome home!" A husky man with straight brown hair and a tidy mustache entered, and a familiar odor wafted past Skye's nose. The man's green T-shirt and jeans bore a layer of dust and straw. Sweat beaded his forehead, and his feet were covered with poor excuses for white socks. *I know that smell*, Skye told herself. *It's like Flanagan's barn two foster homes ago.*

Skye clenched her teeth. Life was moving so fast that her head spun like a ceiling fan. Yet her outside oozed "cool." She'd been down this road too many times before.

"So—your name is Skye?" the man asked, shaking her hand. "I'm Tom Chambers. You can call me Mr. Chambers, Mr. C., or Dad."

Though it was clearly the friendliest greeting she'd ever had, Skye yanked her hand free from his and stuck her thumbs in the back pockets of her jeans.

"Not in this lifetime," she said.

"O—kay, I'm glad to meet you, too!" Mr. Chambers kidded. Then he turned and gave Mrs. Chambers a kiss on the cheek. "How was your day, dear?"

"Very interesting," she said. "Did you find the frozen beef stew?"

"Yep. Morgan has it simmering on the stove. Right?" He looked at the girl listening intently in the wheelchair.

"Yes, sir. Supper's just about ready," Morgan replied, turning her chair and heading to the back of the house.

"Looks like the van needs to be emptied," he said, glancing out the open door.

"Let's eat first," Mrs. Chambers suggested. "Then while you bring in Skye's things, I'll show her around." She walked toward the kitchen. "This way, Skye. Supper will be ready in ten minutes, Tom. After we unpack, it'll be time for Skye's surprise."

After supper, Mr. Chambers unloaded the van, while Morgan cleaned up the "special needs" kitchen: spacious floor, low counters, pots on low hooks, faucets accessible to kids in wheelchairs.

Humph! was the only word Skye's brain could muster since compliments of any kind were not part of her vocabulary. Still, she caught herself staring as Morgan maneuvered with ease in the kitchen.

"Skye, come with me." Mrs. Chambers pushed away from the table and headed down a long hallway. While she spouted off about this bedroom and that room and how they'd all be filled during summer camp and blah—blah—blah—Skye planned how to get control of her life again. In addition to restricted use of the TV, there were ridiculous limits on the phone.

Skye paid little attention to Mrs. Chambers' words until they reached the end of the hallway, and she heard, "This is your bedroom."

Bedroom. My bedroom? Yeah, right. My bedroom, Skye thought sarcastically. *Sure.*

She had slept in basements, dens, and even a makeshift "bedroom" over a garage. The only real bedroom she ever remembered was big enough for two, but it housed three sets of bunks.

"We want you to have some privacy," Mrs. Chambers said, turning toward Skye. "This is *your* bedroom and no one else's. I'm sure that's different from other foster homes you've been in. We'll respect your privacy as long as you don't give us any reason not to." She winked before opening the last door on the right.

Like a book cover to a fairy tale, the door revealed a room with a single bed dwarfed in a white spread so fluffy it looked like a summer cloud. Strangely, there were no curtains on the two windows, allowing the late afternoon sun to bathe everything in gold dust. Dark hardwood floors gave the room a look of royal elegance. Despite there being no pictures on the walls or decorations on the dresser or desk, Skye was impressed. Aware that her mouth had just fallen open, she snapped it shut and plunged her thumbs in her pockets to cover up her delight.

"As you can see, it's nice and roomy," Mrs. Chambers said. "As for the curtains, pictures, and things like that, we were sure you'd have some ideas of your own. We'll go shopping soon, and you can pick out some things that would make this room just right for you, including another bedspread if you don't like this one. By the way, you can unpack later. First there's someone I want you to meet."

Skye's pout took hold again as she followed Mrs. Chambers down the long hallway into the living room. *Now what?*

"Okay, Tom!" Mrs. Chambers yelled.

Skye heard a door open and before her next breath, two small white dogs tore into the room, barking, jumping up against her legs, squealing, and squirming.

"Get them away from me!" Skye screamed as she flopped backward into a cushioned chair, pushed herself further back into it, and kicked at the dogs. Her outside "cool" completely vanished, overtaken by a panic that screeched from her voice. "I hate dogs—they're dirty—and they bite!"

"Here, boys," Mrs. Chambers ordered as she relaxed onto the sofa. Both dogs launched themselves next to her, wiggling, barking, and licking her face.

"Skye," Mr. Chambers said as he entered the room, "you're only afraid of things you don't understand. Dogs are some of the friendliest creatures God put on this earth. Their one desire is to please us." He sat next to his wife, patted the dogs, and scratched their backs.

"I don't care," Skye replied. "I hate dogs."

"They won't hurt you," Mrs. Chambers said. She stood up and held her hand shoulder high. Both dogs hopped to the floor and watched her hand without moving a muscle.

"Now watch," she continued. "Dogs can be trained to obey your every whim. There's no need to be afraid of them, particularly West Highland terriers. They love kids, especially girls. Skye, meet Tippy Canoe and Tyler Too, better known as Tip and Ty."

One dog sat on his haunches, raising his front paws like he was praying. The other one walked on his hind legs in a circle and barked.

"Aren't they adorable?" Mrs. Chambers asked. "Say hello, boys."

A barrage of friendly barks echoed off the walls until Mrs. Chambers lowered her arm. The dogs sat down.

"In about three days, they'll desert Morgan and start looking for you at bedtime," Mr. Chambers said. "They love the new kid on the block. If you don't become bosom buddies, it won't be their fault."

Skye stared viciously at the dogs. "Was this the big surprise?"

"No, that's out back," Mr. Chambers said.

Mrs. Chambers added, "I think it's time you meet someone very special."

Skye could hardly take another surprise. The last month had been full of surprises she could have done without: thrown out of one more foster home, battling Judge Mitchell, juvie hall again, stuck in another strange place with more strangers who were going to "help" her, attacked by two wild beasts, and now what? To her this all seemed like one big, cruel joke orchestrated by none other than Hannah Gilbert. *Wouldn't she just be thrilled to death to see me in this fix?* Skye fumed.

"Come on, Skye," Mrs. Chambers said as she walked toward a sliding glass door in the dining room. "Let's go outside. Morgan, we'll finish the dishes later. Come with us." She slid open the door.

Mr. Chambers led, followed by his wife, one red-haired girl in a black wheelchair, two white dogs, and a juvenile delinquent with her face as fire red as her T-shirt and fists stuffed in her pockets. The wooden deck outside led them down a long wooden ramp onto a sidewalk. The parade made its way down a gentle slope through a velvet lawn to a white fence enclosing a red barn and spacious pasture.

The afternoon sun had already given way to evening shadows, and the air now felt crisp and damp. Everything had a pinkish cast to it that made it look like a Saturday morning cartoon. A strong "Flanagan's barn" smell permeated the air.

Skye felt like screaming as she brought up the rear. She hated following directions, and she double hated being last. It didn't matter how nice this place was. She had to get out of this trap. But how? Dark thoughts pulled her face into hateful contortions.

"This is ridiculous!" she yelled. Her words fell on deaf ears as everyone focused on the large meadow on the other side of the fence.

Skye slowly approached the fence, scanning the field before her. In the distance, near a pond and under a clump of trees, stood a small herd of horses.

Mr. Chambers leaned on the fence with his elbows, stuck his fingers in his mouth and released a shrill whistle.

Skye stepped back, glaring intently as the horses lifted their heads and started running toward the fence. They came up the gentle slope, manes and tails flying in the breeze. *One, two, three, four, five, six!* Skye counted as she backed further away. As they charged toward the barn, Skye focused on the horse in the lead, smaller than the rest but fast as the wind.

The rumble of their hooves on the ground took Skye back to when she was younger, alone in bed during a terrible thunderstorm, and she backed onto the sidewalk. "Just what I need to make my day perfect," she yelled. "Stinking horses!"

Mr. Chambers crawled onto the top of the fence just as the herd came to a sliding halt in front of him.

"I'll get their oats," Mrs. Chambers said, unlatching a chain around the gate. "Stay!" she ordered Tip and Ty as she squeezed through the opening and hurried into the barn. Both dogs retreated, lying down next to Morgan.

Mr. Chambers jumped into the pasture and singled out the lead horse from the cluster now shuffling in front of the barn. Snapping a rope into the halter, he maneuvered it outside the fence, and closed the gate.

From inside the barn, Mrs. Chambers slid open a big steel door, and single file, the other five horses hurried in.

Morgan backed up, pivoting her chair to watch what would happen next.

"Skye, this is Champ, our registered sorrel Quarter Horse. We call him Champ because he is one. The big bay mare is his mother, Pepsi," Tom said, pointing toward the open barn door.

"Champ, meet Skye."

The horse nodded three times, then let out a whinny that edged Skye back a few more feet.

You only fear things you don't understand. Mr. Chambers' words echoed in Skye's mind. But the hotshot juvenile delinquent *was* afraid. She had always hated and avoided animals, especially big ones. And this thing was so—*big!* Now there was no escape. Skye scanned the creature from head to tail as she stood glued to the ground.

Slowly, Mr. Chambers led the horse closer to where Skye stood. Champ inched forward and reached his head toward Skye.

Skye stiffened, ready to back away again.

"Don't move. He's sniffing you," the man said. "He won't hurt you. Champ is one of the sweetest hunks of horseflesh I've ever known."

Hanging on the man's words, Skye tried to relax but felt her knees starting to shake. Brave? Put Skye Nicholson up against any human, male or female, and she'd throw the last punch. But animals? Horses? She was a bowl of Jell-O. "Does he bite?" she asked sheepishly.

"Only apples, and I think he can tell you aren't wearing one."

Gently, the horse inspected Skye's bare arms, snorting, and then he licked her with his warm, sticky tongue. It felt clean and moist.

"Let him smell your hands," Mr. Chambers said. He pulled the rope gently to lift the horse's head.

Skye crept her hands out of her pockets and opened both palms under the horse's muzzle. The horse sniffed and snorted, and then licked her again. Amazed, Skye released a tiny giggle. It was the first time she could remember laughing in an awfully long time.

"What's he doing?" she asked.

"He's getting to know you. I'll tell you right now, he likes you a lot. He doesn't nudge his muzzle up to just anybody. Yep. He likes you a lot."

Skye found herself with strange, new feelings. She had never touched a horse. She hated animals, or at least she thought she did. Her short stay at the Flanagans consisted of watching the cows from the back porch of the house. But now, deep inside, she felt a warm glow as she looked into the deep brown eyes of this gorgeous, friendly animal.

Animal? This is no animal, Skye told herself. *It's a horse— the most beautiful one I've ever seen.*

Its sharp ears pricked forward as if it could read her mind. A white stripe ran down the middle of its face, and its soft mane and tail blew in the breeze like corn silk. Its reddish brown coat, sleek and smooth, sparkled in the sun. And the smell? Like sweet, fresh-mown hay.

"Can I touch it?" Skye asked.

"He's not an 'it.' He's a gelding," said Mr. Chambers. "That's a male horse that's been fixed so he can't reproduce. It takes the wildness out of them. Sure, touch him, but move slowly. I'll hold his halter. Pet him on the nose and feel how soft he is."

Skye inched her right hand forward and stroked the warm nose while the horse licked her other hand like a lollipop. The soft furry hair felt like a velvet pillow. For that moment, Skye forgot who she was, where she was, or even why she was here. She was speechless.

"He's a good one, all right," Mr. Chambers said. "Only fourteen and a half hands high. Just the right size for you."

"Me?" Skye shrieked. "No way!"

Chapter Three

Settling into a new foster home was as exciting to Skye Nicholson as math homework. In five minutes, she had unpacked her beat-up suitcase and tossed her world's possessions into three dresser drawers. Most importantly, she had unpacked a tiny tablet of ragged notepaper and a lighter—both tucked away in rolled-up socks. The tablet was her lifeline to good times—phone numbers of "friends" who helped her get pills or pot to make it through each miserable day.

Living with a new set of strangers and all their rules made Skye so anxious that she felt like throwing up. She glanced at the darkness outside the window and then looked at her watch. Only 9:30. Skye belly-flopped across the bed and closed her eyes.

One day down and a few dozen to go before I'm history, she told herself. *Then I'll move on to the next nightmare.*

Someone tapped on her door a few times before opening it. Mrs. Chambers carried in a bunch of baby pink roses stuck in a shiny brown vase. Tucked under one arm were a navy blue sweat suit and some kind of stuffed animal.

"Skye," Mrs. Chambers said, placing the vase on a desk in the corner, "I want to officially welcome you to our home."

When her new foster mother sat down beside her, Skye rolled away, placed her hands behind her head, and stared at the ceiling.

"I know you've been through an awful lot," Mrs. Chambers continued. Skye didn't say a word. "I want you to know we're here to help you. With God's help, you can make it, kiddo."

God? You've gotta be kidding, Skye thought. *If there is a God, he's sure not interested in me. I'll give it a month before I'm shipped off to the next rat hole.*

"We have a lot to talk about," Mrs. Chambers said, trying again to communicate. "But it can wait until tomorrow. You look like you're ready for bed. We all get up at six o'clock around here, so you need to get some sleep."

Skye flew up into a sitting position without ever moving her hands. "Six o'clock? No way!"

"Yes, way," was Mrs. Chambers' flat reply. "We have devotions and chores before we even start breakfast. We'll explain all of that tomorrow morning. I'll warn you ahead of time. If you don't get up, you'll feel ice-cold water dripping on your face. So be prepared!"

Skye flopped back on the bed, pinched her lips tight, and stared at the ceiling again. *Devotions? Not in this lifetime.*

"Tomorrow will be busy for all of us. Mr. Chambers will talk to you about homework, chores, riding the horse, and—well—you'll see. You and I are going to yard sales and the mall. You'll need something nice to wear to church on Sunday. Let me guess. You've never worn a dress and don't plan to. Right?"

Skye turned her head and scowled at her foster mother.

"Thought so," Mrs. Chambers said. "A nice pair of dress pants and a new blouse will do just fine."

Church! Skye looked back at the ceiling. *Yeah, I remember going to church once. They stuck me in a class with a bunch of brats. Good cookies—rotten kids. Then there was Samantha, the screwball foster mom. Church to her was wearing a white robe, stringing flowers in her hair, and dancing with her other fairy friends under a tree somewhere in the middle of nowhere. Church. Yeah, right!*

"I am *not* going to church!" Skye said, glaring at Mrs. Chambers.

"Surprise! You *are* going to church. It's part of your court order. The judge knows how invaluable church is to any young woman. Give it a chance. You might even like it. There are lots of kids there your age."

From behind her back, Mrs. Chambers whipped out a stuffed bear in a cowboy suit—ten-gallon hat and all. Whirling as though hung from puppet strings, it danced and then disappeared to the right. Skye shifted her glance to the woman who held the bear in a warm embrace.

"Skye, I'd like you to meet Dude. Until you accept Tip and Ty, Dude can be your best friend. Now I'll warn you ahead of time, he won't do well bouncing off walls or having his head stuck in the toilet bowl, but he'll love sleeping with you when you feel lonely. I've never known a girl who didn't have a horde of stuffed animals. I didn't see any with you, so Dude can be your first."

"Don't be ridiculous!" Skye sassed. "I'm not some baby who plays with dolls."

"Believe it or not, I made this critter," Mrs. Chambers said, ignoring Skye's remark. "Every foster daughter has gotten one of my creations. Besides riding, it's my next favorite way to relax. Do you sew?"

Skye snorted. "No way."

"Anyway, he's yours," Mrs. Chambers said softly. As she stood, she placed the bear next to Skye. Then she held up a navy blue sweatshirt with MARANATHA spelled in rainbow letters across the front and a matching pair of sweatpants.

"Since you're now an official client of the Maranatha Treatment Center," Mrs. Chambers said, breaking into a bright smile, "you've also earned the right to own this double-duty, not-your-ordinary Maranatha sweat suit." She imitated a barker at the state fair. "Use it for riding, doing dishes, or sleeping. It takes you places in high fashion. All for the small price of puttin' it on, this can be yours today."

Skye just glared at her.

"It's a little warm right now to sleep in this, but it's yours," Mrs. Chambers said. She folded the sweats and placed them next to the bear. "Would you please sit up for me? What I want to say now is very important."

An agonizing long pause finally forced Skye to sit up. She folded her arms defiantly.

"Please look at me," Mrs. Chambers said.

Finally, Skye gave in and glared at her.

"I want you to know that I love you—we all love you—and we're glad you're a part of our family now. You've already noticed there are no bars on the windows or locks on the doors. You're free to run, but running will never solve your problems. If you face them head on, you can conquer them. That's why you've been sent here, so you can get the help you need. If you do run, I promise you with no reservations, we *will* find you. The only way you'll ever leave here is if we decide it's time for you to move on to something better. Until then, you are our official daughter, and we'll treat you that way—no matter what."

Skye was dumbfounded, but she didn't let it show. On the outside, she still looked tough as nails. Had she actually heard the word *love?* No one in her thirteen miserable years had ever said that and really meant it. And the gifts? The last time Skye had gotten gifts was four foster homes ago from "Uncle Ken," who wanted something in exchange. She didn't want to think about it.

What does she really want? Skye wondered. She stared deeply into Mrs. Chambers' blue eyes.

The woman walked toward the door. She bent down, switching on a nightlight with a prancing horse on the glass cover. Grabbing the doorknob, she turned back. "Good night, Skye. Pleasant dreams."

The door gently closed, and Skye flopped back on the bed. Her sleepy eyes studied the bear and sweat suit. She yawned and shifted her gaze to the roses on the desk.

What's with the presents anyway? she asked herself. *She must want somethin'.*

Skye kicked off her sneakers and crawled under the spread without even thinking about changing her clothes. Clicking off a lamp on the nightstand, she grabbed the bear and held him at arm's length in front of her drooping eyes. The softness of the nightlight illuminated the bear's face enough to make it look like he was smiling.

Pow! For some reason she didn't understand, Skye punched the bear so hard in the nose that his ten-gallon hat went flying across the room. Holding the bear up, she waited, wishing he would cry, but the room was quiet.

Without warning, her own eyes flooded with tears. She tucked the bear tightly against her chest. Those horrible feelings—being alone at night, unwanted, and scared to death—were there as always. But tonight she didn't feel so terribly alone. She had this stupid bear—Dude.

With another lonely tomorrow to face, she curled up into a tight ball around the bear, buried her face against his fur, and cried herself to sleep.

Chapter Four

Early Saturday morning, Skye awakened to the loudest marching music she had ever heard. Sure enough, her watch said 6:00 a.m. She covered her head with a pillow and went back to sleep. The next thing she remembered was cold water dribbling on her face.

"Hey!" Skye barked as she launched herself up, scowling at a smiling Mrs. Chambers.

"Good morning, Skye!" Mrs. Chambers said as she backed toward the door. "It's Saturday, and we have a full day planned. We don't want you to miss out on any of the fun. Mr. C. is waiting for you at the barn."

"Fun?!" Skye snapped.

Mrs. Chambers left and gently closed the door.

While Morgan and Mrs. Chambers made breakfast, Skye slouched out to the barn where Mr. Chambers showed her what chores she would be responsible for every day, including scooping horse poop!

"Of all the thousands—no millions—of foster homes, I wind up in one with you stinking hay munchers that poop on your floors *all* night long!" Skye complained. "This place stinks! You stink! And life stinks!"

Later after showering, Skye slouched to the breakfast table and sat down with three weird strangers.

"Let's pray," Mr. Chambers said.

Skye refused to bow her head and tried to ignore his long list of thanksgivings. *Chesterfield is looking better every second*, she moaned inwardly.

"And, Lord, we thank you for this food and the hands that prepared it. Amen," he said, and then reached for a large bowl filled with yellow fluff. "Ah, my favorite. Scrambled eggs, toast, and juice to start a beautiful spring morning. What about you, Skye?"

"I'd rather have a Pop Tart," she grumbled.

Mrs. Chambers passed a plate of buttered toast. "You're probably not accustomed to eating breakfast, but it's an easy habit to form."

"Yeah," Morgan added as she poured juice in four glasses and passed them. "I remember before I came here, all I ever scarfed down in the mornings were Twinkies and donuts. No wonder I was bonkers! Sugar brain!"

"Donuts sound pretty good to me," Skye said, barely scooping out one spoonful of eggs. She forced herself to take a piece of toast from the passing plate.

"Today is going to be an exciting day for Skye," Mrs. Chambers said to the family. She spread apple butter on her toast. "After devotions she and I are going to yard sales and the mall. Morgan, would you like to call Rita? I'm sure you can spend the day over at her house."

"No thanks, Mrs. C.," Morgan replied. "I have a big report due on Monday, and I want to clean my room before I get arrested for aiding and abetting dust bunnies."

How in a zillion years can she clean her room in that thing? Skye asked herself, glancing over at Morgan's wheelchair. *What a priss!*

"Hey, how come you're in a wheelchair anyhow?" Skye asked.

"I was born with cerebral palsy," Morgan answered.

"But that's never stopped her from enjoying life, has it?" Mrs. Chambers added and then directed the next question to her husband. "What do you have planned today, dear?"

Mr. Chambers sipped his juice. "I'll be doing my 'Home, Home on the Range' thing today. I need to bale the hay I cut in the south field this week, and the lower pasture fence needs mending. Maybe Skye would rather help me than go shopping." He chuckled.

Mrs. Chambers laughed. "What's your preference, Skye? Pitching hay bales in a barn loft or choosing new clothes and bedroom accessories. The choice is yours."

Skye grimaced. "Shopping," she answered as though she would rather not do either.

"We'll be back some time in the late afternoon," Mrs. Chambers added, sipping on a cup of coffee. "This evening

I'll show her around the property. So, Skye, whenever you're ready, we'll hit the road."

After tackling every yard sale in a thirty-mile radius, Skye and Mrs. Chambers ate lunch at Skye's favorite fast-food place and then visited the interior decorating department of the largest store at the mall.

"I hope you've put some thought into your bedroom and what you'd like to do with it," Mrs. Chambers said. She and Skye walked slowly up and down the aisles.

"Not really," Skye answered casually, trying to hide her excitement at the thought of actually making some decisions on her own.

"What do you like? I mean, do you have any hobbies—anything that interests you?" Mrs. Chambers pointed to a wall display littered with bright colors and designs. "Look at all those different spreads and matching curtains."

Skye studied the display, searching for something different.

"A while back I saw the coolest movie," she said, "and this girl had a black light and dark purple walls with long strings of glass beads hanging on the windows. That was too cool, but I don't see any black spreads here. Maybe we could get some posters at the gift store I saw when we came in."

"No, I don't see any black spreads either," Mrs. Chambers said. "Anything else you like?"

Skye stood thinking, her mind far away, and a half smile slipped out. "Hey, I know! Mr. Johnson, you know, my last foster dad, raced dirt bikes. He had the coolest red bike. I always wanted to ride it, but he'd never let me. Yeah, dirt bikes. I love dirt bikes! And motorcycles— really big ones—like Harley Davidsons."

"Now we're getting somewhere," Mrs. Chambers said, pointing. "Look there! That teal and beige one with—I don't believe it—red dirt bikes. That set looks like it was made just for you."

Skye rushed toward the wall display and pulled the large plastic bag out of a bin. "Wow, this is too cool! Can I get this one?" Her face beamed with delight.

"Sure," Mrs. Chambers answered, smiling, "and I imagine that gift store has some really neat posters with dirt bikers flying all over dusty roads. Very good, Skye. You'll have the coolest bedroom this side of Snyder County. Let's check out, and we'll go back to the gift store."

"Sweet!" Skye said, following Mrs. Chambers.

After supper with the family, Skye could hardly contain her excitement when she put on a helmet and climbed on the back of a four-wheeler behind Mrs. Chambers.

Wow! This is more like it! Skye thought. *Forget the horses, and sign me up for this!*

Together, they toured Keystone Stables, with Mrs. Chambers revealing some interesting facts that even caught Skye off guard. The place was more than a foster home. It was also a licensed facility for kids with all kinds of problems. Those who were deaf, blind, and had other special needs were all welcome at the thirty-acre ranch for weekends and summer camps. Everywhere she looked, Skye saw ramps, railings, and different kinds of equipment.

Beyond the fences and pond were open fields and riding trails through the woods and hills.

To the right of the pasture, a short distance from the house, Skye saw a cluster of towering pine trees with a gazebo, picnic pavilion, and a trickling brook with a wooden bridge. To the left, behind the barn, sloped a gentle hill with a breathtaking view of more rolling hills, farmland, and Jack's Mountain off in the distance.

As the sun was setting, Mrs. Chambers and Skye pulled up to the back of the house on the four-wheeler.

"There's one part of our house you haven't seen yet," Mrs. Chambers said. "Our basement is not exactly an 'ordinary' basement. I'll show you."

Skye followed Mrs. Chambers around to the side of the house to an entrance with a flashing business sign above the door that said CHAMBERS' CHAMBERS.

"This is Tom's business, Skye. He builds and repairs computers," Mrs. Chambers said, as they walked into a room that looked like a small computer factory. "Over in the other part of the basement is our game room."

Mrs. Chambers flipped a light switch and opened a door.

"Wow!" Skye exclaimed. Her glance darted from one end of the spacious room to the other. The wall on her right was stacked with a television and DVD, CD player, computers, and video games, as cool as any arcade she had ever seen. A Ping-Pong table and pool table stood in the center of the room. And tucked in the back was a kitchenette with a serving counter. To her left along the wall stood a row of card tables and folding chairs. In the far back corner hung a lamp on a chain that looked like a traffic light with red, yellow, and green lights.

"It's yours," Mrs. Chambers said. "All you need to do is ask."

"Really?" Skye asked.

"Really."

Saturday, one of the best days of Skye's life, came and went too quickly. Reality hit her square between the eyes on Sunday when the family attended Community Bible Church. As far as she was concerned, it was just another painful experience she'd have to endure. In Sunday school teen class, Skye super-slumped in a chair next to Morgan.

During the main worship service, Skye double-super-slumped between Mr. and Mrs. Chambers, trying to ignore everything Reverend Newman, the man in the fancy suit at the pulpit, said. It didn't make any sense anyway. Heaven? Hell? Forgiveness? Jesus dying for the sins of the world? It was like a foreign language to Skye, and her mind wandered as far away as she could get.

Of all the tortures prepared just for her, the one that shook Skye the most was the one facing her on Monday, the first day of her ten-day suspension from school: riding the beast Champ out in the field.

To make matters worse, both Mr. and Mrs. Chambers took off work to spend the day with Skye, showing her the ins and outs of living with horses.

Morgan had just left for school, the sun was splitting the sky, and Skye found herself marching between her prison wardens and two guard dogs off to the gallows at the barn. What she wouldn't give now for a ticket to Chesterfield. Her only other option was faking appendicitis, but she wasn't sure where her appendix was, so instead she grumbled all the way to the barn.

"Now," Mr. Chambers said as he unlocked the corral gate and all three walked through, "we're going to take this easy. First we'll show you how to handle a horse with your feet on the ground."

Skye watched the dogs as they took off, sniffing the ground, running back toward the house. She glanced down in the meadow. A cluster of horses ate grass near the pond's edge. Inside the corral, she backed up against the closed gate, hung her thumbs on her pockets, and tried to steady her legs. Frantically, her eyes searched for a hole to crawl into, but there was none. She ran her fingers through her hair, never letting her glare leave Mr. Chambers. He opened the barn door, grabbed a lead rope off a hook, and walked into the shadows.

"We'll help you get to know Champ before you ever get on his back," Mrs. Chambers said. "You'll do just fine. Just relax. He can sense when you're nervous."

Skye snarled, "This is ridiculous! I don't want to—I can't—"

"We're here to help you. Just give yourself a chance."

Out of the shadows came Mr. Chambers leading the sorrel gelding. Skye studied the horse from head to tail as the two approached. The morning sun bounced off his reddish-brown coat, making him look like he had been polished with expensive oil. Champ's muscles rippled as he pranced, and his mane and tail whisked in the breeze. Scared as Skye was, she was overwhelmed by the beauty of this magnificent horse. Now, suddenly, her wobbly legs had some competition—a melting heart and half a will to at least try to get to know this gorgeous beast.

"I'll get the grooming gear," Mrs. Chambers said, disappearing into the barn.

"Hold your hand out, and let him sniff you," Mr. Chambers said, leading the horse closer to Skye.

Skye cautiously reached out her hand, surrendering it to the horse's muzzle.

"Now, come and walk up here with me, Skye," Mr. Chambers said as he faced the horse toward the side of the barn. "Don't ever walk behind a horse, no matter how well-trained he is. That's dangerous. Always stay where he can see you, either far enough in front or to his side."

Mr. Chambers waited for Skye, and then the three walked on until they reached a metal brace on the wall, where he tied the rope.

Skye stood a safe distance away, studying every move the horse made as Mr. Chambers positioned him.

Champ nodded three times, rubbed his head on his leg, and whisked his tail to shoo a fly. Then he looked directly at Skye and forced out a loud whinny that made her jump and step back further.

"Here we are," Mrs. Chambers said as she rounded the corner. "Now we'll show you how to keep a horse clean."

Skye sidestepped toward Mrs. Chambers and fixed her glare on every move the frisky animal made.

"This is a currycomb," Mrs. Chambers said, lifting a round metal-toothed tool out of a bucket followed by four other items. "And this is a comb for his mane and tail, a brush, a hoof pick, and insect repellent. Since he's not covered from head to toe with mud, we'll start with the brush. Here." She shoved the brush into Skye's unsuspecting hands.

"You want to ride a happy horse?" Mr. Chambers said as he held Champ by the halter. "You groom him before *and* after you ride him. Never mind the fact that after you're done he'll roll in mud or dust on the field. He still loves to be brushed. Come on. I'll show you what to do."

As though walking on glass, Skye stepped toward Mr. Chambers and tried to hand him the brush.

"Oh, no," he said, "you do it. See the strap on the back of the brush? Slip your hand through that and step up to his side."

Skye did as she was told, lips pinched, knees wobbling, heart melting.

"Start up by his ears and under his mane. Brush in long strokes as hard as you can. When you get better at this, you'll have a brush in both hands. Now go ahead. Work your way down his neck, withers, and across his back and rump. Then we'll do his other side and the legs."

Skye took a deep breath and stepped toward the horse, holding the brush out as if it were poison. Just as she carefully reached up and laid the brush on his neck, Champ moved his hind legs, shifting his rump toward her.

Skye jumped away from the horse, and she felt like she was going to jump out of her skin. Her cheeks flushed and the hair on the back of her neck prickled.

"I can't do this!" she insisted.

"Sure you can," Mrs. Chambers said, slipping her arm around Skye. "Here. I'll help you. One thing you need to remember is that Champ is highly trained. I know that doesn't mean anything to you now, but once you get to know him, you'll be amazed at how obedient he is."

The woman clicked her tongue and placed her hand on the horse's rump. He sidestepped back against the barn and stood without moving a muscle.

Together Mrs. Chambers and Skye approached the horse. This time Skye passed her test, placing the brush on the horse and swiping numerous times across the whole side of his body. As she finished brushing his rump, Champ looked back at Skye, letting out a soft nicker that sounded like he was giggling.

"What's that?" she asked.

"That was Champ's way of saying he approves," Mr. Chambers said. "He really does like you. No doubt about it."

"Here, use this on his legs where the mud is caked on." Mrs. Chambers handed her the metal-toothed tool.

Skye bent down, noticing crumbly pieces of mud on all four legs near the hooves. Using the comb, she scraped off what looked like hard icing on a stale donut. "How did that get there?"

"The sweetest grass in the meadow grows down at the pond's edge," Mr. Chambers said. "When the horses go after that treat, they get all muddied up. Horses and mud go together like ham and eggs."

For an hour, the Chambers showed Skye how to groom Champ, how to clean his hooves with a pick, how to comb his mane and tail, and how to apply bug repellent to his coat. They even showed Skye how to use an electric razor on Champ's ears, muzzle, and legs.

They also told her about the seriousness of feeding hay and oats properly—the right amount at the right time or there could be deadly consequences.

"A horse's digestive tract is *very* sensitive. Colic is a dangerous ailment to a horse," Mrs. Chambers said, "and founder can kill a horse, so we must be extremely careful about food and water."

Skye had just finished brushing Champ and was just beginning to feel half confident about the horse thing, when Mr. Chambers came out of the barn carrying a western saddle, blanket, and a bridle.

Oh, no, she thought. *I'm not ready!* "I—I—need to use the bathroom," she said to Mrs. Chambers.

"No problem," Mrs. Chambers replied. "There's one in the barn near our office. Come on. I'll show you."

You have to be kidding, Skye grumbled. *No way am I gonna get outta this!*

In a few minutes, Skye was back, facing her uncertain future. As she stared at the horse now equipped with saddle and bridle, visions of one scared silly kid with long dark hair flying into the side of the barn flashed through her mind. This was it. Her life was over. *Good riddance*, she thought.

"We'll show you how to saddle and bridle him another time," Mr. Chambers said as he loosened the horse. "Come here, and I'll show you how to lead him."

Skye did as she was told—barely.

"Now," he said placing the reins in Skye's hands, "you lead a horse from the left side since that's the side you usually mount from. Put your right hand up close to his muzzle and hold tightly to the reins with your other hand." He showed her and then put the reins into her hands.

Skye squeezed so tightly her knuckles turned white.

"Relax, honey," Mrs. Chambers said.

"Would fainting be relaxed enough?" Skye sassed.

"That's a good one," Mr. Chambers said as both he and Mrs. Chambers laughed.

"I didn't mean it to be funny," Skye grumbled, pumping out a sarcastic half-smile as she stood glued to the ground.

Mr. Chambers walked to the right side of the horse. "Now I'll lead Champ from this side. You just walk along with us. We'll stay in this small corral and walk in circles. We'll stop and turn him several times so you get the feel of the reins. Ready? Just click your tongue. And when you want to stop, pull gently on the bridle. He's trained to stop on a dime. God made a horse's mouth very sensitive. It doesn't take much to stop him with that bit in his mouth, so be careful. Did you know it tells us in the Bible that a tiny bit controls a powerful horse like this one? God's Word has wisdom for every facet of life, even how to handle God's creatures."

What is he talking about? Skye asked herself. *The Bible? What does that have to do with horses?*

Over and over, Skye practiced leading Champ around the paddock. She learned how to get him to start and stop and how to tie him to a post. She also learned that she could "ground-tie" this well-trained horse. No post or brace around? Just drop the reins to the ground and he stayed put, rain or shine, day or night.

"It's ten o'clock, Tom," Mrs. Chambers said as she leaned on the corral fence. "How about a coffee break? Skye, how about a snack?"

"Good idea," Mr. Chambers said. "Skye, tie Champ to the barn like I showed you. After the break, you'll be ready for your very first ride."

Take a break? Skye panicked. *Yeah, I'll take a break. I'll probably break my neck!*

Chapter Five

Skye's break hardly lasted long enough for her to catch her breath, let alone plan an escape or come up with a good lie to get out of riding the horse. One thing she'd noticed about the Chambers was that they never let her out of their sight. *I'm dead*, she moaned inwardly.

While they sipped coffee and told her how great she did, Skye nibbled off a few chunks of an apple and then laid it on her napkin while she pictured herself in a coffin. The more she thought about it, the more frantic she got, running her fingers through her hair and staring into space.

"Well, I think it's time," Mr. Chambers said. "Ready to go, Skye?"

Mrs. Chambers pushed away from the table. "You go ahead while I clean up," she said, picking up the mugs. "Don't worry, Skye. You'll do great. I can tell by the way Champ responds that you two will hit it off. You can do anything you put your mind to. I love Philippians 4:13: 'I can do everything through him who gives me strength.' You should try that one on for size."

I am so sick of this God stuff, Skye thought. *God! He doesn't even know I exist.*

Skye followed Mr. Chambers back out to the barn, hating it more than before. "I can't believe this," she grumbled, biting hard on her lower lip.

But now Skye started to argue with herself. *I did learn to brush the horse, and I did learn to lead it—no, him. Maybe—.*

"Here," Mr. Chambers said as he came out of the barn with a round black object about the size of a bowling ball. "Put this on. It's a hardhat to protect you if you fall. State regulations." He gently positioned the helmet on Skye's head and snapped the chin strap closed.

Oh, great! she thought.

"When we show, the hardhat is standard attire with English style," he said with a mock English accent. "You'll see me wearing one when I jump with our thoroughbred Diamond over those walls down there."

Skye looked in the direction he was pointing and saw three gray-colored fieldstone walls in the lower field.

"Of course, when we Westerners dude up in our plaid shirts and chaps for shows," he said with a cowboy drawl, "we wear authentic cowboy hats. When you kids practice Western, we think these look kind of funny."

Mr. Chambers gently tapped on Skye's hat. "But I guess a ten-gallon hardhat would look funnier. It's for your protection anyway," he said in his normal voice. "If you take a tumble, this little hardhat could save your life."

"Great," Skye complained. "Now I not only feel stupid, I look stupid too!" She tugged at the unfamiliar chin strap and swiped her hair back from her face.

Skye slipped inside the gate as Mr. Chambers untied Champ and led him in front of her. Standing in front of the horse's muzzle, he tugged gently at the bridle and clicked his tongue.

Skye studied every move the horse made as he shifted into a stand like a Marine private called to attention. With legs straight, neck arched, and body like a statue, Champ presented a picture of perfection.

"What's he doing?" Skye asked.

"He's squaring up," Mr. Chambers answered as he dropped the reins and stepped back. "We told you this horse is intelligent and well-trained. In his five years, he's been in all kinds of competitions and has blue ribbons to prove it. Show horses must learn to stand like this while the judges look them over. This is as easy as we can make it for you to mount. He won't move a muscle until you're ready. Are you ready?"

"I—I—guess so," Skye squeaked.

Mr. Chambers retrieved the reins, placed one on each side of Champ's neck, and then gathered them at the saddle. "All right, come to the left side and put your foot in the stirrup." He pointed to the large leather loop dangling from the saddle.

Skye's wobbly knees dragged her to the horse's side. And with her teeth embedded in her lip, she reluctantly placed her right foot in the stirrup.

"Whoa! The other foot! If you mount that way, you'll be driving his tail!" Mr. Chambers laughed and pointed to the front of the saddle. "Now grab the reins and the horn and with your other hand grab the back of the saddle."

"Horn?" Skye shriveled up her face in a question mark.

"That little knobby thing that sticks up on the front of the saddle. English riders call it a pommel."

Skye did as she was told, even though panic caused her eyes to widen and body to shake. "Tell him not to run!"

"He won't run. Now up you go!" Mr. Chambers hunched down and pushed his right shoulder under Skye's backside, launching her straight up onto the horse.

"I don't want to do this!" Skye cried as she plopped into the saddle.

Mr. Chambers grabbed the cheek strap of the bridle, ignoring Skye's objection. "When you learn to ride English, you'll put one rein in each hand, but you're learning Western style now. Put both reins in one hand, and keep the other hand on the horn. He's been trained to neck rein. All you have to do is lay the reins on either side of his neck, and he'll turn. Got it?"

"Yessss."

"Now, stick your foot through the other stirrup. Let me see if it's the right length." Mr. Chambers checked a strap underneath Champ's leg. "Fine and dandy. Your legs should be slightly bent like this, and your feet should rest comfortably in the stirrups—the front part of your feet, that is. When you get a good pair of cowboy boots, it'll be much easier to keep your heels where they should be, in back of the stirrups and down.

"Now I'll lead Champ. You just hold the reins loosely. Whatever you do, don't pull hard. Let him have his head. I'll be right here beside you. Ready?"

"Noooo," Skye said, sitting on the horse like she had been starched.

"Relax!" Mrs. Chambers yelled from the fence. "Let Champ do the work. You just enjoy the ride."

"Since he's so well trained," Skye said sarcastically, "can he brush his own teeth?" She squeezed the horn like she was trying to open a brand new jar of pickles.

"Skye, you crack me up," she laughed. With Mr. Chambers leading and Skye hanging on for dear life, Champ walked as slow as a turtle inside the corral.

"Hold him! He's gonna run! Hold him!" Skye screamed.

"You're doing great!" Mrs. Chambers encouraged her.

Around they walked, stopping, turning, and walking again. On the outside, Skye was a scared rabbit hanging on for dear life. On the inside, her heart was melting!

"I hate this! I hate animals! I hate . . ." Skye paused, struck by the realization that she was riding a beautiful show horse! She felt proud and free as a bird.

"Wow!" she yelled. "I can do this! I can really do this! Hey, look, everybody! I'm riding a horse!"

"Way to go, Skye," Mr. Chambers said as he continued leading her in a circle.

"Ride 'em, cowgirl!" Mrs. Chambers yelled. "I knew you could do it!"

A shot of courage surged through Skye. She released her hand from the horn, reaching cautiously toward Champ's neck. Gently, Skye crawled her fingers under his thick, flowing mane and stroked his coat, which was warm from the rays of the sun—as warm as her not-so-nasty heart. She took a deep breath and smiled.

"Good boy, Champ," she said. She felt herself becoming part of the horse, part of something she thought she hated. "You are way cool!"

Over the next few days, the Chambers monitored Skye while she spent hours on Champ, riding him in the corral, learning to saddle and bridle him, brushing him, and loving him. The "I-hate-animals" part of her had been replaced by a glow inside that drew her to the beautiful horse, as well as to Tip and Ty.

"You're a natural-born rider," both Mr. and Mrs. Chambers said as they taught Skye. By Friday she was out in the pasture learning to ride while Mr. Chambers used a longeing line on Champ. Already she knew how to use her legs to shift the horse's weight while jogging in circles. "Left lead! Right lead! Back him up! Use your knees!" She had never been given so many orders in such a short time, but now she didn't mind. She didn't mind at all.

On Tuesday afternoon while Skye stood in Champ's stall brushing him and combing his mane and tail, Morgan motored into the barn with a bridle on her lap and a lead rope in her hands. She was headed for one of the stalls.

Skye paused and leaned out over the bottom half of the Dutch door, watching her pass. Finally, overcome with curiosity, she said, "Hey! What's up?"

Morgan stopped and turned her chair toward Skye. "Tuesday's one of my days to give Blaze a workout. We're getting ready for the horse show in August."

"What do you do? Walk the horses, brush them, or what?"

"Duh!" Morgan jested as she poked her index finger in her cheek and made a face. "What do you think I do? Just sit in this chair 24/7? The dun mare down in the last stall is mine."

"No way," Skye laughed. "You can't be serious. How can you ride a horse?"

"Come on," Morgan said. "I'll show you." She headed toward the end of the barn.

Skye slipped through the half door and placed the currycomb in a bucket outside the stall.

"I only need a little help with the gear, and then, of course, getting on," Morgan said, swinging open the wooden gate to Blaze's stall. "Here, Blaze."

The horse gently stepped in front of Morgan and lowered her head into the girl's lap. Morgan clipped the lead rope on Blaze's halter and motored out of the barn with Skye following far behind them.

Outside Morgan tied Blaze to a post next to a wooden ramp and platform with railings that looked like a porch with no house. Skye watched as the horse squared up like she had probably done a zillion times before.

Mr. Chambers came around from the back of the barn carrying a blanket and a strange-looking saddle with a high horn and a higher back. He placed them on Blaze, tightening the cinch.

"There you go, Morgan."

Skye watched Morgan motor up the long wooden ramp onto the platform and position herself to put the bridle on Blaze.

"Do you want to help?" Morgan asked.

"Sure, why not," Skye said. "What do you want me to do?"

"Check on the other side to make sure the brow band is on correctly around the ears, okay?"

"Okay," Skye said, making sure the bridle fit correctly. She glanced under Blaze's head at Morgan. She still couldn't quite believe this disabled kid was going to ride a horse without falling off.

"Ready, Morgan?" Mr. Chambers asked.

"Yep."

Mr. Chambers gently lifted her from the wheelchair into the supportive saddle and secured her legs tightly with two Velcro straps on each side of the horse.

"Huh," Skye said, watching Morgan jog to the center of the field. The warm-up exercises were even more impressive, but Skye was blown away when Morgan completed a barrel race in lightning-fast time.

"She's something else, isn't she?" Mrs. Chambers said, joining her husband and Skye as they leaned against the fence. "Ask her to show you the ribbons on display in her bedroom. Most of them are blue."

"No kidding," Skye said.

Skye's ten-day suspension seemed to fly by. Never had she enjoyed a school suspension so much, even with all the uncertainties and the fact that she was missing her friends. She couldn't help thinking that getting suspended again or expelled for that matter would be a cool idea. Then she could spend all her time with Champ.

The warmth of Saturday's sun released the sights and smells of a perfect spring day. The horses frisked about in the pasture, running down to the pond, chasing and nibbling at each other. And now, not even two weeks after she first touched a horse, Skye found herself on Champ, following Mrs. Chambers and Pepsi on a dirt road in back of the pond.

"You know, Skye, it's nothing short of a miracle the way you've taken to horses," her foster mother said as she led the way along a trail through the woods. "Are you sure you've never ridden before?" Mrs. Chamber's blue eyes smiled from beneath a suede Stetson hat.

It had been a long time since Skye had told a big lie just for the sake of telling one. She needed practice, and now was the perfect time. "Well, I did know how when I was little, but I forgot," she answered curtly.

"Oh, I see," Mrs. Chambers replied. "Well, relax and enjoy the ride," she added. "I'm going to give you a crash course on trail riding. Ah, maybe I should rephrase that. I'm going to show you the ins and outs of trail riding. Without the 'crash,' that is. And I want to show you a very special place. Bring Champ up here. There's no need for you two to follow us. The road is wide enough for both horses."

Skye clicked her tongue and confidently rubbed her calves along her horse's belly. With a hop, Champ started jogging, coming alongside Pepsi and matching her pace. It was like being in the best movie Skye had ever seen. Brilliant shafts of sunlight lit up budding trees of pink and white blossoms, squirrels chattered, and birds chirped.

It was so peaceful that words would have ruined the magical moment. The clip-clop of the horses' hooves on the dirt road, the jingle jangling of the bit shanks, and the squeaking of the leather saddles said it all. Skye hated to admit it to herself, but she was having the time of her life.

Finally, Mrs. Chambers spoke. "You know, I've never gotten over the thrill of riding a horse down a path in the woods. I think it's about as close as you can get to heaven. God made all this beauty, kiddo."

Skye cringed. She reached down and patted the horse's neck. Champ she liked—no, *loved*. But Mrs. Chambers? Just a necessary inconvenience to get what Skye wanted.

The long trail through the woods led into a small pasture nestled at the base of three sloping hills. Blossoming trees dotted the field that overflowed with tawny grasses. Skye focused on a covered wagon in the center, nestled under a clump of sassy scrub pines. As the horses swished their legs through the tall grasses, a gentle breeze stirred, sifting the smell of pine through the meadow.

"Wow," Skye said. "This is *so* cool."

"Welcome to Piney Hollow," Mrs. Chambers said as they approached the wagon. "Let's rest awhile."

The horses walked to a wooden railing, one of several on the side of the wagon, as if they knew just where to go. Mrs. Chambers and Skye dismounted, wound the reins around the railing, and walked to a clearing that included a circle of rocks for a campfire surrounded by wooden crates to sit on.

"I bet you're wondering what goes on here, aren't you?" Mrs. Chambers asked. "We use it for trail rides, camping trips for our church youth group, and special chapel services when the weather permits."

"Chapel services?" Skye's face contorted, weighed down with all kinds of questions.

"Look over there." Mrs. Chambers pointed to something behind Skye.

Skye turned and focused on several rows of benches hewn from tree trunks. In front of the benches, set against the sharply rising base of a hill, was a monument of cemented stones about as tall as the wagon with a beautifully carved stone cross projecting from the top.

"That's our chapel. We've had a lot of church picnics here. You haven't lived until you've eaten a hot dog or marshmallow roasted over an open fire."

Mrs. Chambers tapped on Skye's hardhat. "Why don't you give your head a rest and take that off?"

Skye gladly took off the hat and ran her fingers through her sweat-dampened hair. She plopped down on a crate across from her new foster mother.

"Isn't this place a sight for sore eyes?" Mrs. Chambers said. "It amazes me how God gives us the desires of our hearts. I never knew serving him could be like this. Tell me about your other foster homes, Skye. Which ones did you like the most?"

"There's nothing to tell," Skye said. "I hated all of them. Sometimes I felt safer at juvie hall."

"Well, we hope you feel safe—and loved—here."

"At first I thought you were trying to kill me when you put me on him," Skye said, nodding at her horse. "But riding Champ isn't so bad. It's pretty cool."

"We're praying you'll think living here is pretty cool too, and you'll be able to call our place 'home.' We'd like nothing better," Mrs. Chambers said as she stood. "I guess we've rested enough. Let's take advantage of a perfect day. We can talk while we ride through the woods."

Skye was glad their little chat was over. This God talk was getting on her nerves.

Chapter Six

The restrictions Skye faced at the Chambers' home offset the freedom she experienced whenever she rode Champ. And to make sure she remembered the rules, Mr. and Mrs. Chambers had reviewed them with her every evening the first week she had moved in.

"Well, Skye," Mr. Chambers said as he stirred cream into his coffee, "how do you think you're doing with all these rules we have here at Keystone Stables?"

Skye nibbled on a brownie and took a big gulp of milk. "The only difference between here and juvie hall is you don't make me wear those stupid khaki uniforms. I hate those things. They make me feel like a private in boot camp."

"Honey, we want you to understand one thing," Mr. Chambers said. "We have rules for one basic reason—so you'll feel safe. You might feel like you're in a straitjacket now, but believe me, as time goes by, you'll get used to them. And after you've lived here a while, we won't need some of them anymore. You'll be so used to the other ones, you'll think life has always been like this."

"The only thing I figure is that you're getting ready to ship me off to the Marines," Skye complained. "Actually, that would be like a vacation."

Mr. Chambers chuckled and wiped his mustache with a napkin as he pushed his cup aside and reached back to the counter to retrieve a paper. "Let's go over this list one more time. If you want to discuss any of these, just speak up."

A barrage of barks echoed from Tip and Ty, who sat on the floor between Mr. and Mrs. Chambers.

"Not you two," Mrs. Chambers said. "Whenever they hear the word 'speak,' it sets them off like robots with new microchips."

Skye grinned in spite of herself.

"Okay, here we go," Mr. Chambers said.

Skye folded her arms, slid into a half slouch, and rolled her eyes. "I can hardly wait," she grumbled.

"Careful," Mrs. Chambers warned.

Mr. Chambers started reading:

"Use of the playroom, including computer games, e-mail, and TV—one hour a day under close supervision."

Skye stared passively at a brownie crumb.

"Boom box and CDs—Christian music only."

Gag a maggot, she thought.

"Phone—one ten-minute call a day under close supervision."

My life is so *totally ruined.*

"Chores, including the house and the barn—washing clothes, ironing, housecleaning, cooking, gardening, and mucking stalls. But you're not a lonely island out there by yourself," Mr. Chambers reminded Skye. "It takes all of us to run this place. It's just part of maintaining a home. You'll be glad when you're older that you learned how to do these things."

Yeah, I'm the luckiest girl in the world! Skye stewed on the inside.

"Skye, you're a beautiful young lady. It's important to have proper personal hygiene, not only for your health, but it keeps flies out of the house." Mrs. Chambers laughed gently. "Of course, that means a shower, including shampooing your hair every day, brushing your teeth twice a day, and trimming your nails with scissors rather than biting them off. From the looks of those gnawed-off nails, you could use some finger etiquette. And remember to change your underwear and socks every day."

Skye rolled her eyes again. "Could you get any grosser?"

After having the rules drilled into her night after night for a week, she could hardly forget. Nonetheless, she fought them like a badger in a bag. She would run the shower and sit on the vanity, while gallons of water ran down the drain—just so they would think she was doing the wet thing. Rules were made to be broken, she reasoned, and she was there to break every one. How else was she going to have a little fun?

Although hostile to the Chambers, Skye studied Morgan with calculated interest. She thought she saw another teenager with a kindred spirit who could join in her rebellion and help buck the system. Or so she thought!

The first evening after the school sent assignments home, Skye answered a knock at her bedroom door and invited Morgan in. A tower of books was stacked on Skye's desk, waiting.

"Mrs. Chambers mentioned that you had homework," Morgan said as she motored in. "Suspension doesn't mean a vacation!"

Skye sat on her bed, hands behind her head, feet stretched out and crossed. She eyed Morgan as she entered, escorted by Tip and Ty, whose toenails clicked on the floor until they settled on a throw rug beside the bed.

"Yeah, big deal," Skye answered. "Those books can sit there until they turn to dust. I'm not doing it."

"What do you mean you're not doing it?" Morgan asked. "Don't tell me you're one of those poor little mistreated foster kids who claims she can't read. Get a life!"

"Yeah, I can read, but only things I like. When it's too cold for me to bum around downtown, I go to the back room of the city library, hide in the corner, and read neat stuff. Nobody ever bothers me. Sure, I can read, but not that trash." She nodded toward the desk. "Anyway, I'm *not* going to do homework just because Mrs. Chambers says I have to. How can you stand all their stupid rules?"

"They're not that bad," was Morgan's encouraging answer.

"Yeah, right. Of all my foster homes, this is the weirdest! What really bugs me is this God thing all the time. It makes me sick. How long have you been here, and how can you stand it?"

Morgan raised her eyes as though she were reading from the ceiling and then looked back at Skye. "It'll be three years this summer. I had just turned twelve when my parents got divorced. Dad left us and ran off to California with another woman. It was too much for Mom. She had three other normal kids to support, so I landed here. Mom's always been a little unstable. If the Chambers hadn't taken me in, I'd probably be in an institution somewhere."

"Do you ever see your parents?"

"Not Dad. He has a new life, he says, and doesn't see any of us. Mom moved closer to Aunt Martha down near Philly. She calls every now and then. I did see her and my brothers and sister last Christmas, but they only stayed a few hours. They're really not like my family anymore. The Chambers are more like parents to me. Do you ever see your parents?"

Skye blurted out a sarcastic laugh. "That's a joke. I don't even know where they are or if they're even alive. I've been in foster homes as long as I can remember. They don't want me, obviously, or they would come and get me. I don't know a stinking thing about them, good or bad." Skye's tone changed. "So you're in ninth grade at Madison?"

"Yeah. Next year I learn to drive."

"Learn to drive? In that thing?" Skye snickered and pointed to the wheelchair.

"Sure. Why not? Lots of challenged people drive. You've seen me ride a horse, haven't you? Why can't I drive a car?"

"But how?" Skye's face contorted.

"We have a really neat van with special gears and pedals up in the dashboard to use with your hands. It is *so* cool. I'll have to show it to you sometime."

Skye's face grew serious. "Now that you've mentioned Madison, do you know Sooze Bodmer—it's really Sue—and Kenny Hartzell? They're seventh graders."

"Nah. High school kids never have any contact with kids in other buildings. Why?"

"I need something from them. Fast. They're my *special* friends, if you know what I mean."

"Look, kid, that kind of stuff won't fly around here. I'm telling you, Mr. and Mrs. Chambers will find out. You'd better not pull any stunts like that."

"C'mon, Morgan. You can do it. If you can't connect with my friends, get some stuff from somebody in your class. I need it to get me through this nightmare. A weed or two—speed—anything! What do you say?"

Morgan's freckled face grew as serious as Skye's. "I say you're just plain stupid, Skye. Are you on any hard stuff?"

"No!"

"Well, that's a plus. At least you won't suffer withdrawal. But I guarantee you *won't* be doing any kind of drugs here. Look, I'd like nothing better than for us to be friends," she said and then smiled, "even though you *are* a lowly seventh grader. But I won't get you any stuff."

"Why not?"

"'Cause I don't do drugs anymore. Skye, my life really changed when I moved in here. With the Chambers' help, I learned about God. I accepted Christ as my personal Savior, and he helped me kick all my bad habits. I don't have anything to do with those kids anymore."

"Not you too! I can't believe it! You're a religious nut? C'mon. Couldn't you just smuggle me in a beer or somethin'?"

"Not in this lifetime! With the Chambers' and God's help, you can change and get rid of those things that are messing you up, too."

"I am *not* messed up!"

"Have you looked in a mirror lately?" Morgan taunted.

Skye's face flushed hot, and she raked both hands through her hair. "You mean you're not going to help me?"

"Yeah, I'll help you, but only with things like your homework. Forget that other stuff. It's your call if you want to be friends."

"Thanks for nothing," Skye growled and folded her arms tightly across her chest.

"And you are *so* not welcome," Morgan said, as she motored to the book pile on the desk. "Look. We have hours of work ahead of us. Let's get started." She grabbed the top book and opened it on her lap.

"I am *not* doing homework, Morgan, so you can just forget it!"

"Hey, listen. I'm just trying to help. If you don't do this, you'll lose privileges."

"Privileges?" Skye whined as she sat up straight and tucked her knees to her chest. "What privileges? All I need is a straitjacket, and my life will be complete."

"I'm telling you for your own good. You've only spent a few hours at Maranatha since Monday, right?"

"Yes-s-s-s-s-s . . ."

"Well, the individual counseling and group therapy can be intense, to say the least. Then there are your riding privileges here at Keystone Stables. Are you sure you want to give up Champ for a week at a time? I can tell you're already hooked on him."

"No way. Just because I don't do this stupid homework?"

"Duh! Yes with a capital Y—E—S!"

Skye just sat there.

Morgan reached toward the desk, searching for something. "Your assignments should be here somewhere. Here they are," she said, pulling folded papers out of a book. "Well?"

Skye's face shriveled like a dried-up prune. *Maranatha? Big deal. I can take anything they dish out to me. But lose Champ?*

"Okay!" she snarled. She shuffled to the edge of the bed, scaring the dogs out of her path. "If you're dumb enough to waste your time in here, I'll do it. But, hey, don't offer to do me any more favors. I made it on my own this long, and I'll make it on my own again. Got it?"

"Man, you've got a lot to learn and not just in school," Morgan snapped as she motored toward the bed.

Chapter Seven

Skye thought the awfulness of living with the Chambers paled in comparison to what she suffered at Maranatha Treatment Center. The place was *the pits* as far as she was concerned.

She had a long history of counseling with tons of psychologists who had tried to figure her out. But Maranatha was different. It was a Christian counseling center supported by local churches and run on a shoestring budget. On the very first day of her suspension, Skye discovered her manipulative strategies wouldn't work there. The place crawled with weirdos like Eileen Chambers. Mrs. Chambers had taken a reluctant Skye from room to room meeting the staff.

"Skye," said Mrs. Chambers as they walked into the front office, "I'd like you to meet Fred Scott, our program director. The Marines weren't tough enough for him, so he decided to tackle this job."

Mr. Scott pushed his dark muscular frame away from his desk, stood, ran one powerful hand over his crew cut, and reached the other one toward Skye. "I'm glad to meet you," he said. His brown eyes sparkled behind thick-rimmed glasses.

Skye stuck her dead-fish hand in his. "Yeah," she said.

Mrs. Chambers pointed to an adjoining room with a desk and computer. "That's Mrs. Klase, our secretary, and our van driver, Mr. Boyer."

"Hello, Skye!" Mrs. Klase yelled as her stubby fingers pecked at a keyboard. Her stare never left the monitor.

"Howdy do," Mr. Boyer said.

In the next office, Skye met an older counselor named Alan Ling, who was from some Asian country.

Then there were the ten to fifteen kids like her meandering down the hallway or gathering in a large open room. At last, Skye had found kindred spirits. Red, yellow, black, and white slouch champions, sass experts, highbrow liars, druggies, tire slashers, and hooky players. Skye felt at home. She might have to suffer through group counseling, but at least she had company.

Every day after that, Skye met with Mr. Scott and the group in a room large enough for a circle of metal chairs to hug the center and cafeteria tables to line the walls. This was Interactive Instructional Counseling, better known as IIC. Mr. Scott and other adults lectured about drugs, pregnancy, parents, and other supposedly important issues. Then after a week of the same boring stuff, Mr. Scott changed the routine.

As usual, Skye sauntered off the van, complained all the way into the building, and sought out her new friends in the large room. Just like clockwork, fifteen minutes before the session began, Mrs. Klase served boring snacks while the group mingled, consoling each other in their miseries.

Spiked-hair kids with earrings in their noses and eyebrows, girls with Gothic makeup and black clothing barely covering their bodies, and boys with elephant-size T-shirts and cargo pants dragging on the floor grabbed their snacks and slinked to the corners in little cliques. Bad attitude seethed in the room—except for two girls who were dressed much like the others but stood talking and half-smiling with Mrs. Klase.

Skye melded into one of the corners and practiced her own Oscar-winning pout. But on the inside, all she could think about was Champ.

"Ladies and gentlemen," Mr. Scott's gruff voice announced. "Gather around, please. We have no special guests today. It's Melissa's turn to bring herself up." He gestured toward the girls standing with Mrs. Klase. An attractive blond looked at the floor as her face turned bright red.

Bringing herself up. Ha! Mrs. Chambers had told Skye about this new type of therapy. Today Melissa would stand before the group and come clean about her latest "sins." If everything went as planned, she would be grilled by the rest of the group about what she'd done wrong. Then Melissa had to say she was sorry. That's when Mr. Scott and the other kids would tell her how great she was.

"No way!" Skye had said after hearing about it. "Why would anyone in their right mind 'fess up to a bunch of kids who are doing the same things? That's stupid."

"It takes a lot of courage to admit you're wrong," Mrs. Chambers had said. "You'll see. And we can't even begin to help you until you get to that place."

Now Skye found herself mumbling and dragging herself to the center of the room with all the other kids. She flopped onto a chair, grumbling under her breath, and waited for the sideshow to begin. In the meantime, she spent the moments dreaming about Champ and devising a plan to kidnap him and leave her miserable, rotten life here behind.

"Before we start"—Mr. Scott's voice raised as he pushed his way forward—"I have some announcements. Settle down, please."

They all settled in their own good time.

"First of all, will the person who blocked the toilet with paper towels please come forward?"

A hornet's nest of snickers erupted from the circle.

"All right, quiet down. You may think you're getting away with something, but we'll eventually find out who you are, and you *will* face the consequences."

Begrudgingly, the nest of kids settled down.

"Secondly," Mr. Scott continued, "Umlauf's Bakery called yesterday. Anyone at least fifteen years old want twenty hours of work a week?"

More dissension erupted.

"Hey!" he said, almost shouting, and the mob quieted. "Look at it this way. Twenty hours a week in programming or twenty hours a week earning megabucks. Think about it."

"I also want to remind you that after IIC and pizza today, we're going bowling for our weekly activity. Remember, people, no hiding in the bathrooms and smoking, no couples snuggling in a corner somewhere. You will all stay with the group. Is that clear, ladies and gentlemen?"

"That's it for announcements," Mr. Scott said over the quieting rumble. "Now today is special for Melissa." He pointed at the girl now sitting sheepishly across from Skye. "Melissa has come a long way in her six months here. She's learned about responsibility, blame—and—well—Melissa, come up here."

Melissa stared at the floor, folded her arms, and stood next to the man.

"Why are you here today?" asked Mr. Scott.

"I'm bringing myself up."

"Okay, people. You heard that. She's bringing herself up. Please give Melissa your undivided attention."

Like magic, as soon as the words left Mr. Scott's mouth, every kid sat silent and focused on Melissa.

Skye slouched, watching the others. On the outside, her cool eyes surveyed the circle, while on the inside her mouth dropped open. *Wow! What's happening?*

"Okay, Melissa. You have the floor," Mr. Scott announced.

A panic-stricken Melissa slowly faced each kid in the room. Skye studied the scene, her eyes darting from Melissa to the other stone faces in the group.

"I'm bringing myself up because I snuck out of the house at midnight last week and ran away. I know that was wrong." Her lips quivered as her fingers played with the short sleeves of her too-tight top.

"Why did you do that?" a teen with a head of tiny braids barked. He folded his arms and sat more erect in his chair.

"Because my old man—I mean my father—was drunk again."

"Unacceptable!" the girl with the nose ring snapped. "Just because your old man was drunk, you ran away?"

Mr. Scott stepped forward. "It's 'father,' not 'old man,' Pam."

"All right—*father*," Pam answered. She smacked while chewing a giant wad of bubble gum. "C'mon, Melissa. Tell us why you ran."

Skye gawked at them all. *Man, this is tough*, she thought. *No way am I ever gonna do this. No way!*

Melissa's face reddened even more and her eyes filled with tears. "'Cause I'm afraid of him when he's loaded."

"Yeah, but why didn't you call Maranatha?" shouted a pudgy girl with a shaved head and ears lined with silver studs. "You know that's what you're supposed to do when you're in trouble. That's the deal we made."

"Yeah!" the entire circle repeated in sarcastic slurs before they all fell silent.

Tears ran down Melissa's face. "I know I should have called instead of running away with Marty," she sobbed, wiping her eyes with both hands. "That's why I'm here. I know what I did was wrong. I'm asking you to forgive me."

The circle of kids went silent.

"Did you hear that, ladies and gentlemen?" Mr. Scott said. "She's coming clean. She made a mistake, and now she's here to make things right. It takes a lot of courage to do that. What do you say? Shall we forgive her?"

Without hesitation, every kid, including Skye who followed the rest, gathered around Melissa. Boys extended their hands to shake hers, some girls patted her on the back, and others hugged her.

"We forgive you, Melissa," Pam said.

"You did good," the guy with the braids said. Others echoed with "you're okay now," or "we're with you all the way." IIC was over, and Melissa smiled.

Skye stood back, totally shocked by what she had seen. Never before had she witnessed anybody 'fess up and really mean it—in front of a group no less! She studied Melissa's peaceful, relieved face. Maranatha was definitely different. But Skye hadn't decided whether that was a good or bad thing.

Mr. Scott spoke above the chatter. "Please be seated. Except you, Melissa. Stay here."

He gestured for her to stand next to him and then whispered in her ear. She nodded. The group fell silent.

"Melissa has something else she'd like to say," Mr. Scott added. "Go ahead, Melissa."

With still glistening eyes, Melissa now beamed with new-found hope. "After they found Marty and me last week, I realized that what I've been learning here at Maranatha is the truth. I decided to come clean not only with the staff here but also with God. I accepted Christ into my life, and he's helping me see things a whole different way. He's becoming the best friend I ever had. I wish you all would try it. It's so cool."

"I think from now on you'll see a whole different Melissa," Mr. Scott said. He shook Melissa's hand warmly. "Welcome to the family of God."

I can't take much more of this God stuff, Skye thought. *When I run, nobody's gonna find me!*

Three times a week at Maranatha, drug and alcohol counseling forced Skye into what she considered her own private torture room—Mrs. Chambers' office.

"Get off my back!" Skye had complained at her first session. "I don't need you raggin' on me. I'm not hopped up on drugs!"

"Maybe you're not on the hard stuff," Mrs. Chambers said, "but any kid who needs a handful of uppers a day needs help. And that includes you."

After that, Skye had nothing to say.

Still, she had to face individual counseling again on Friday. After IIC, pizza, and bowling, all but three of the others had been dropped off at home. Both Mr. Scott and Mr. Ling had retreated to their offices with their clients, and that left Skye alone with Mrs. Chambers.

Skye's emotions ran wild. On the outside, she was seething with hatred. On the inside, she just wished everyone would vanish into thin air.

"Well, Skye," Mrs. Chambers said as she folded her hands on the desk, "is today going to be different, or are we going to meditate for an hour? You know I'm in this for the long haul. We'll meet as long as it takes to tackle your problems. If you'd start talking, you'd realize that hope and solutions are available. What do you say?"

Mrs. Chambers smiled, and Skye looked down. As usual when sitting before this woman, Skye's heart pounded like a drum and her stomach did back flips.

Afraid? Of Mrs. Chambers? Yet, there was something in Mrs. Chambers' smile and in her deep blue eyes that caused Skye to feel conflicting emotions. She detested sitting in this office alone with her—and yet she liked it, although she would never admit it. Somehow Eileen Chambers was different. Despite the stupid rules and all she stood for that Skye hated, Mrs. Chambers really did seem to care.

Skye wrestled with her feelings. She'd felt this conflict between liking and hating before. It hadn't worked in the past, and Skye was sure it wouldn't work now. She had tried liking—no loving—her foster mom four homes ago. Skye had handed her heart to Mrs. Taylor on a silver platter. What a mistake! When she discovered that all Mrs. Taylor wanted was a baby-sitter for the twins, Skye's heart had been ripped out like a button off a rag doll.

On the other hand, why not have a little fun? Skye thought. *Tell a few dozen lies just to get it over with. Why not? I have to sit here anyway.*

Skye looked up into Mrs. Chambers' pleading blue eyes.

"Is that a yes?" Mrs. Chambers asked.

Skye nodded and gave a stingy this-ought-to-be-good smile as her heart slowed a little and she found herself relaxing into the chair.

"I think that after a while you'll find that you actually enjoy these sessions." Her eyes darted from Skye to the paper and back. "All we're going to do is chat, so take a deep breath and relax. I'm just going to ask you a few questions. For the last two weeks we've been discussing how important it is to confront your fears. Remember?"

Skye nodded and ran one hand slowly through her hair.

"I've read your court records, and for a thirteen-year-old kid, you've been through an awful lot. Can you remember how many foster homes you've been in?"

"Four, five. I don't know," Skye forced out.

Mrs. Chambers gently opened Skye's file. "According to this, you've been in thirteen foster homes and never longer than six months. How do you feel about that?"

"I hated every one of them," Skye said.

"Hate drives people to do terrible things. Do you know what hate is?"

Skye felt her heart pound a little faster before she answered. "It's when you can't stand something so bad you could throw up, punch somebody's lights out, and run away all at the same time!"

"Did any of those things ever make you feel better?" Mrs. Chambers asked.

"Throwing up did and so did the other two until I got caught!"

"But did they solve the problem?"

"Nah."

"What causes people to hate, Skye? What causes people to lie, to murder, to do bad things?"

"Bad vibes, raw deals—a rotten life that's not fair. I've had my share!" Skye said.

Mrs. Chambers reached for a book on her desk.

Skye's eyes followed her every move. *Not the Bible! Here we go again*, she groaned inwardly.

Mrs. Chambers laid the book down and then leafed through it. "Did you know the Bible tells us that Satan is the father of lies? He's the enemy of God and the originator of sin. That includes hate, deceit, murder, and all evil. What do you think of that?"

Since we're talking about lies, I'll demonstrate. Time for a lie—a big one, Skye thought.

"For real," she said with a charade of interest cloaking her face. "I never knew that. So it isn't really my fault, is it?" Skye knew about that Satan stuff from Mr. Rice, five foster homes ago. Most of the time she didn't buy it. But sometimes she could feel something—anger, rage, hate—when she listened to hard rock or took certain pills. Who knows? Maybe it was Satan's power. Just thinking about it gave her the creeps.

"Skye, your hate is your own fault," Mrs. Chambers said, relaxing in her chair. "According to the Bible, we're all responsible for our own actions." She leaned back and smiled. "What do you think of your parents?"

"I hate them!" Skye's voice rose emphatically.

"How can you hate someone you don't even know?"

"I just do. That's all. Can we change the subject?" Skye's posture stiffened and her face flushed.

"It's going to take more sessions to deal with this issue, Skye. But before we wrap this up, I want you to realize one thing. Although you are totally responsible for all of your actions, there's a reason behind it. You are so full of hate for your parents that you can't see straight. Did you know that anger and bitterness can destroy you?"

Skye shook her head and slouched in disgust.

Mrs. Chambers' voice softened. "Skye, when you allow bitterness to fester in your heart, it eats away at you just like a cancer. Eventually, it will destroy you and deeply hurt all those around you. The only way you can get rid of it is to ask God to take it away. That's why you're stuck in a cycle of hate. That's why you do drugs and run away. You need God to clean all that hate out of your heart and fill it with love—his love. Skye, are you listening?"

"Yeah," she said weakly. But she was thinking. *Not in this lifetime! My parents can rot for all I care.*

Chapter Eight

With her suspension finally over, Skye dragged herself off the yellow school bus in front of Madison with what felt like a ton of books and two tons of homework. She hated this place! Besides suffering through the homework, her frazzled brain had been working overtime on this foster home business. If it weren't for Champ, she'd be history!

Trudging up the concrete steps, Skye scanned the hallway packed with rowdy middle schoolers, banging locker doors, chattering with each other, hurrying, laughing, and scowling. Weaving her way to her locker, she searched desperately for two familiar faces.

Sooze and Kenny, where are you? I just have to see you before I report to Bubba's office. I just have to!

"Hi Skye," said a sweet voice from behind.

Skye turned toward the girl who had grabbed her arm. "Oh, hi!" Skye said.

It was Robin Ward, one of the few people Skye could stand at Madison. Robin had short dark hair. She was built like a bulldozer, yet sweet as sugar. Robin was an honor roll student and a star softball, basketball and soccer player. Skye hated to admit it as she looked at Robin's short stocky frame, but she was actually glad to see her, even if she was a little different.

Different? It never occurred to Skye until that very moment that Robin was different because she was like the Chambers! She was one of them. A religious nut. A Christian! She had to be different with the things she said and did—and didn't—do!

"Where you been, girl?" Robin asked, pushing her hair behind her ears.

"In prison," Skye grumbled.

"Prison!"

"Almost. I was placed again. This time in the ultimate torture chamber. Speaking of chamber, their names are Tom and Eileen Chambers. Do you know them? They own Keystone Stables about three miles out west of town."

"Nope. Never heard of them. Is it really that bad?"

"It has one good thing, and only one," Skye said, raising her index finger. "They have horses, and I'm learning to ride. That's the only good part, believe me."

"Horses?" Robin exclaimed. "Sweet! I've always wanted to ride horses but never had the chance. So now you're a dude-ette. You go, girl!"

Skye's face shriveled. "Dude-ette?"

"Yeah, you know. They call cowboys 'dudes.' Well, you're a girl, so you're a dude-ette."

"Not cool," Skye said, throwing her gym bag into the locker. Her voice grew serious. "Hey, have you seen Sooze and Kenny?"

"No, I don't see them much," Robin answered, her tone quickly changing. "You know we don't have any classes together."

Robin was still talking, but Skye was too busy searching the faces in the hallway to listen.

"Skye!"

"Huh?"

"Softball practice started last week. The team's looking for a manager. Do you want to do it? It's after school every day until five."

"Can't," Skye said as her attention shifted back to Robin. "I have counseling at Maranatha."

"What's Maranatha?"

"It's a place over on Fifth and Broad that tortures kids like me. I have to go there every weekday for at least a year. They're trying to *help* me," she said sarcastically as she grabbed a book from her locker.

"Oh," Robin said.

"Gotta go. I have to report to Bubba. I mean Mr. Bubbosco." Skye glanced at her watch as she walked away. "If you see Sooze and Kenny, tell them where I am. Okay?"

"Probably won't see them. Our rotation is completely different," Robin said as she turned to walk in the opposite direction. "See you later in gym class."

Skye slipped into the principal's office and sheepishly approached the high counter that kept kids separated from the staff. To her right, four students slouched in chairs lined up against the wall, each face reflecting the thought, *Get me out of here!* Skye scanned them, hoping in vain that one would be familiar. No such luck.

As she waited impatiently for the secretary, Skye planned her new strategy, one that would keep Bubba off her back—at least for a few days.

"Good morning, Miss Nicholson," the secretary bubbled as she approached the counter. "We haven't seen you for a while. Been watching your step, I guess."

Skye gave her a sheepish grin.

"Now you don't need to tell me why you're here," the secretary continued. "You are top priority. Go right in." Poking the button on an intercom, she gestured to a door that was slightly ajar. "Skye Nicholson is here."

As Skye slipped inside the principal's office, she set her latest plan into motion. *C'mon tears. Work for me.*

"Have a seat, Miss Nicholson," Mr. Bubbosco said from behind his humongous fancy desk. He was not smiling.

Skye slid onto one of three chairs lined up in front of the cherry wood fortress. Unsure of her archenemy's mood, she studied the principal's gray eyes that glared back from a thin frame, a balding head, and reading specs riveted to the end of his nose. She waited, wondering what he possibly could say to make her feel any worse.

Mr. Bubbosco, fifty-something going on eighty, was enemy to all students and friend to none. Skye could tell he thoroughly hated his job, but retirement was just around the corner. Hotshot Bubbosco, better known as "Bubba" behind his back, had seen his better days. Ignoring stacks of folders on his desk, he leaned back in his plush swivel chair and folded his hands behind his frayed hair.

"Miss Nicholson," Mr. Bubbosco began, "you know you are here by pure luck. If it weren't for the Chambers, you'd be serving time at Chesterfield. Frankly, I don't know how many more chances this administration can give you. It depends completely on your attitude. Do you have anything to say?"

Skye paused long enough to portray deep thought. *Here we go*, she schemed as she crafted an innocent smile. "Mr. Bubbosco, I'm really gonna try my best this time. Honest. I don't wanna get kicked out of here."

"I hope you're leveling with me," the principal said as though he really wanted it to be true but knew it wasn't. "I know the Chambers will do all they can to help, but you've got to want it yourself. If you don't straighten up, you'll wind up behind bars, so you better get with the program!"

Skye's eyes turned moist. "I—I'm really sorry," she said, lying. "I promise I'll stay outta trouble. I'll . . ."

"Fine and dandy," the principal said, cutting her off. "I'll be watching you. Now get back to class and stay out of trouble." He launched himself forward, his hands shooing her out as his face wore gullible relief blended with a tired smile.

Skye slipped out both doors faster than she went in. She quickly glanced at her watch. Class in five minutes.

"Hey, Skye!" She heard a familiar voice she had longed to hear for two weeks.

"Sooze! C'mere!" Skye said as loudly as she dared and gestured toward the girl shuffling down the hallway.

"I'm coming. I'm coming," said the scrawny girl with big feet and bigger hips. "Where you been?" She punched Skye in the arm.

"In prison! Not really. I've been placed again. It's the pits. When we have more time, I'll tell you all about it. Where's Kenny?" Skye asked, glancing beyond Sooze's short, straight, mousy brown hair, which was sticking out all over as usual.

"Haven't you heard?" Sooze's thin lips and hollow brown eyes answered in disbelief. "He got busted, big time. Last week. Bubba decided a hall monitor wasn't enough. He called in a cop with his sniff dog. They found hard stuff in Kenny's locker. This time his parents couldn't buy his way out. He's been sent upstate for at least eighteen months. Yep. He's doing time for wheeling and dealing." Her arms flung wildly from her cheap T-shirt.

"How about you?" Skye pleaded as she looked behind her shoulder. "I mean—do you have anything?"

"Yeah. Catch up with me at lunch if you want a handful. By the way, you still owe me for the last time." She cocked her right hand and pointed it in Skye's face.

"I know, I know. Just give me a little time. I've been as good as locked up in a box for two weeks. Give me a day or two. I'll get the cash."

"No. I need the bucks at noon today or no deal." Sooze meant business.

"Okay, okay. I'll see you at lunch. Don't forget the stuff."

"Yeah, right. See you then."

As Skye picked at dried-up spaghetti on her tray, she reached under the table and grabbed a small bag of pills from Sooze's hand and slid them into her jeans pocket. "Thanks," she whispered. "These will help me through the weekend."

"Hey, can you get away after school today?" Sooze asked as she consumed a pile of French fries. "Tony will have his wheels. He and Jeff want us to bum around with them at the mall."

Skye's face was suddenly dark. "You know I can't. I have that dumb programming at Maranatha. Man, I really wish I could."

"Bummer!" Sooze said and then guzzled her milk.

"The woman—you know, Mrs. Chambers—said you're welcome to come and ride the horses anytime, and you should see their basement. It's filled with all kinds of neat stuff. We'd be under lock and key, but at least we could hang out together."

"When?"

"She said any weekend would be fine. Just let her know ahead of time and get permission to ride the horses. That's all."

"Cool. I know I can. Mom doesn't care what I do," Sooze said as her gaze swept the noisy room. "Hey, look who's coming this way!"

Skye took a sip of juice as her eyes settled on a knock-out blond dressed in designer jeans, expensive clogs, and a fringed leather vest. She walked like a model down a runway, carrying a full tray and heading straight toward Skye's table. Skye's muscles tensed, and her eyes drew into narrow slits. It was Hannah Gilbert in all of her beautiful, snotty glory.

"Excuse me," Hannah said condescendingly as she placed her tray on the table and pulled coins from her fancy shoulder purse.

"Why?" Skye snapped. "What'd you do?" She and Sooze snickered.

"I'd like to get to that pop machine behind you, if you don't mind."

"No, we don't mind," Sooze barked. "Go right ahead."

"Excuse me," Hannah said, "but *you* are in the way. Would you both move!"

"We are *not* moving," Skye announced as she eyed Mr. Peters, the cafeteria monitor, on the other side of the room. "Why don't you slither under the table?"

Hannah threw her head back and let out a loud sigh. She folded her arms and tapped her foot. "I figured as much from white trash like you!"

Skye's face flushed, and she rocketed out of her seat. Before Hannah knew what was coming, Skye cocked her fist and punched Hannah right in the face, sending her staggering backward into another table.

Mr. Peters came running, yelling at the top of his lungs, "Everybody stay seated! Calm down! No one leaves this room."

Sooze jumped up from her chair with her eyes as big as her spaghetti plate. "Man, are you in b-i-g trouble now! What'd you do that for?"

Skye stood with her fists still clenched like a boxer who was so surprised he won the match he didn't know what to do next. Her mouth was hanging open, her face was flushed, and all she could think of was Chesterfield and never seeing Champ again. Petrified, she scanned the room. Everyone was looking in her direction. The place was as silent as a morgue. A crying Hannah held her bleeding nose, her body quivering in shock.

Skye shoved past Sooze and ran out of the cafeteria before Mr. Peters could reach her table. In the hall, she stopped, took a breath, and looked in both directions. A ray of outside light peeked in as a door opened to her left. Skye tore toward it. As a line of students from gym class filed in, she pushed her way past and ran as fast as she could off the school grounds and down the street toward the center of town.

This time, I'm dead meat, she thought. *Chesterfield, here I come!*

Skye never looked back.

Chapter Nine

Running. It seemed like Skye was always running. Before moving to Keystone Stables, she ran for fun, for the thrill of the chase, just to see if she could get away. Back then she didn't care if she got sent to Chesterfield or any other lockup. Her rotten life was worthless anyhow. But this time it was different. She was running away from Champ.

Skye huddled next to a dumpster at a pavilion nestled between budding maple trees at the city park, her hand clutching the plastic bag full of pills. She continued to pant—not only from running twenty blocks in the May sun—but also from the fear that now gripped her heart. This time running was no joke. She had too much at stake, and if she could undo it all, she would.

"Stupid, stupid!" Pounding her forehead, Skye agonized over her latest stunt. She pulled her knees to her chest and focused on a ball field hugged by a chain link fence and billboards. She pictured Robin running around the bases after smashing a softball over the fence.

Why can't I be like her? Skye brooded. *How can she be so strong, inside and out?*

Skye's thoughts shifted to Hannah. *Miss Prissy deserved to have her lights punched out. But why did it have to happen that way—in front of the whole world?*

Then there were the Chambers and Maranatha. *What will they say? Will they even give me a second chance?*

And what about Champ, the only thing she cared about in the world? She started to cry. *Will I ever see him again?*

Lowering her head between her knees, Skye sobbed until her nose ran freely.

"I told you I'd find you, no matter what!" a familiar voice announced from behind.

Skye felt the plastic bag ripped from her hand, and she jumped as though prodded with a hot iron. She wiped her face, returned her arms around her knees, and then stared at the field once again. She should have known the bloodhound would find her.

"Skye Nicholson, when are you going to stop banging your head against a wall?" Mrs. Chambers asked as she sat down and assumed the same pose.

"How did you find me so soon?" Skye said.

"Contacts in high places, my dear," Mrs. Chambers said sternly. "Are you coming back with me willingly, or do I need to call the police?"

Skye lowered her head, resting it on her knees.

"I take it that means you'll come peacefully. Good." Mrs. Chambers' voice relaxed as she handed Skye a wad of tissues. "Honey, you really did it this time. You'll be facing some tough consequences. I only hope the Gilberts don't press charges. As angry as they are, I'd look for it. If that happens, we won't be able to keep you out of Chesterfield."

Mrs. Chambers gently placed her hand on Skye's shoulder, waiting for a reply.

Skye shrugged off Mrs. Chambers' hand and tightened her pose. "Miss High and Mighty deserved what she got." She blew her nose in the tissues and threw the shriveled-up ball against the dumpster.

"You're doing it again, Skye, blaming other people for your unacceptable behavior."

"Well—she just makes me so mad!"

"One of the reasons you're with us is to learn how to control that anger. When will you learn that your temper causes you nothing but trouble and heartache?"

Skye didn't answer.

"Here's what we need to do," Mrs. Chambers said. "We'll go back to my office. I have phone calls to make, including the Gilberts and Mr. Bubbosco. And I want you to do some serious thinking about what you did. Every day next week, we're going to zero in on your temper. By next Friday, you should be ready to bring yourself up."

"Bring myself up? No way! I won't do that. Ever!"

"The only way we're going to keep you out of Chesterfield is to show the school and the judge that we're making progress. Consider your options. They're pretty limited right now."

A picture of Champ romping in the pasture ran through Skye's mind. She remained silent for a long time.

"Well?"

"All right. I'll try," Skye grumbled.

"That's all I ask," Mrs. Chambers said.

"How about doing some homework together?" Morgan asked as she motored into Skye's bedroom.

Skye, assuming her usual daydreaming pose on the bed, did not answer.

"Earth to Skye!" Morgan glanced at the desk heaped with books. "Let's do some homework. You might have been expelled, but you still have to meet with that tutor at Maranatha every day, don't you?"

"Don't go ballistic on me, Morgan!" Skye protested. "I might as well be locked up in that closet for the next few weeks. I didn't think I'd get the death penalty for such a stupid thing as punching Hannah's lights out."

"Yeah, but you're lucky the Gilberts decided not to press charges. And you better abide by that restraining order the judge issued. As long as you and Hannah don't cross paths, you should be okay."

"Okay? You say *okay* when my life is ruined? No school, no friends. And on top of that, no game room, no phone, and no Champ for two whole weeks in this prison. I can't even walk down to the barn to look at him! Take me out and shoot me!"

"Skye, I told you to be careful. Mr. and Mrs. Chambers are nobody to mess with," Morgan said, flipping back her long red hair. "I had to learn the hard way, too. What restrictions do you have?"

"Only child abuse to the nth degree. That's all." Skye tightened her folded arms and crossed her legs with a snap. "Extra cleaning jobs, double-duty weed picking in the garden, I have to help *you* cook at least twice a week— the list goes on and on!"

"Give me a break," Morgan said. "Look at the bright side for once, will you? At least you're not in jail. You can still play table games with us in the evening."

"Whoopdeedoo."

"And the Chambers included you in last night's Bible study group."

"Double whoopdeedoo."

"And what about the horse show in August? It sounds to me like they expect you to show Champ."

Skye ran both hands through her hair. "Now you've got my attention. If I ever get to see Champ again, will you show me how to practice for the show? He's the only thing that keeps me sane."

Skye returned to her ranting. "Then there's Maranatha. Get this! Mrs. Chambers wants me to bring myself up on Friday. She has got to be kidding. She thinks I'm ready, but is she in for a surprise—a big one!"

"You still don't get it, do you?" Morgan said. "The Chambers and Keystone Stables are the best things that ever happened to you."

"All right, kids," Mr. Scott announced to the circle of slouching, grouching kids in IIC, "today we're going to the Chambers' home. You can play in the game room or take a riding lesson from Mr. Chambers. As usual, no straying from the group, and please get permission to use the bathroom. The main floor is off limits, and I repeat, *off limits*. Is that clear, ladies and gentlemen?"

The grumbling was almost deafening.

"Any questions?"

Mr. Scott turned to Skye and gestured. "Before we go, we have unfinished business. It's Skye's turn to bring herself up. Come here, Skye."

Like magic every kid sat erect and focused on the center of the circle. The room became a tomb.

Skye's hands started to sweat, and she wiped them on her jeans. It was time to run, but where to? And how would she get out? Where could she hide from the group's icy stares and stinging words?

Skye forced herself toward Mr. Scott, her eyes glued to the floor. With her face grimacing in pain, she hugged her chest so tightly she could hardly breathe.

"Okay, Skye, it's all yours," Mr. Scott said.

Skye swallowed hard. "I—I'm bringing myself up because I punched Hannah Gilbert in the face," Skye said in a whisper, still staring at the floor.

"Look at the group, please," Mr. Scott directed. "And speak louder."

Skye raised her head like a bashful child. "I'm bringing myself up because I punched Hannah Gilbert in the face," she repeated a little more forcefully.

"Why did you do that?" someone yelled from behind.

"Yeah," said someone else.

At this point, everything Skye had learned and witnessed in IIC dissolved into thin air. Skye the liar was also Skye the coward. Her pride was still in control.

"I hit her because she made me!" Now no one had trouble hearing her. Skye's face flushed, and her body stiffened with anger.

"She made you?" the boy with the braids chimed. "Cop out!"

"Woo, she made you. Aren't you the big shot!" Pam yelled.

Mr. Scott stepped forward. "All right, people, calm down." He raised his hand toward the group. "Now, Skye, it's time to come clean. Why did you hit her?"

"Because she's a snob, and she deserved it!" Skye answered.

"Unacceptable!" one kid yelled.

"Unacceptable!" added another.

"Yeah. C'mon," a thin boy in front of Skye said. "Don't you wanna make your mother proud?"

"Leave my mother outta this!" Skye demanded.

Mr. Scott raised his hand again, sensing impending disaster. "Whoa. Slow down, everybody. Now, Skye, there's no reason to get so upset about your mother. Tell us a little bit about her."

"Yeah," yelled the bulgy girl with the shaved head "We all have one—or were you hatched?"

Skye's head almost exploded when they started snickering at her.

"Yeah," they all repeated.

That did it. She blew sky high!

"Shut your big mouth, sleaze ball!" Skye screamed. Up went her fists, her face turned fiery red, and she exploded toward the bulgy girl.

The girl launched from her chair, clanging it across the floor, and braced herself for a boxing match that would have ended before it began. One half-hearted blow from the heavyweight girl would have put Skye out for a week—a thought that never entered Skye's mind.

As though escaping from hot lava, the kids scrambled from their chairs, flinging them in all directions, bracing for the rumble of the week. Instantly, a kid on each side of Skye rushed toward her, grabbed her arms, and swooped her up in the air while she swung her fists and kicked viciously. "Let me at her!" she screamed.

"All right! That's enough!" Mr. Scott exploded as he hurdled over the flying chairs into the middle of the group. He grabbed Skye and spun her behind him as he yelled, "Sit down everyone! And don't move until I get back!"

Like spoiled toddlers forced to come in from the rain, everyone grumbled while retrieving their chairs, slammed them in a disheveled circle, and took their time to settle. Mr. Scott was still in charge—but barely.

He spun toward Skye and before her next breath, her arms were pulled behind her, and she was forcibly ushered out of the room, and down the hallway toward Mrs. Chambers' office.

"No!" she yelled as she kicked and squirmed. "Let me go!"

In front of the office, a powerful arm slipped around Skye's waist as another arm reached toward the doorknob. Mr. Scott's foot kicked open the door, and Skye felt herself launched through the doorway and into the chair in front of Mrs. Chambers' desk. Mrs. Chambers shot up from her seat and waited for an explanation.

Mr. Scott huffed as he backed out of the room. "Man, this kid is something else! She can't handle the word *mother*. She just blew it big time. Got everybody mad at her. I gotta get back to the group."

"Thanks, Fred," Mrs. Chambers said quietly. "Please close the door."

As the door closed, the room was silent except for Skye's loud huffing. Gripping the arms of the chair, she stared at the floor, her sweat-soaked hair hanging down over her face. In one vicious swipe she ran her fingers through her hair, returned her arms to the chair, and slid down so low she almost fell in the floor. Mrs. Chambers stared at her in silence and went back to her reading.

In her mind, Skye went over every miserable moment of IIC. Still Mrs. Chambers kept reading. Skye glanced at her watch. Fifteen minutes had passed in total silence.

Mrs. Chambers continued to read, ignoring Skye. Skye repeatedly checked her watch, watching another fifteen minutes crawl by.

Strangely, Skye's rage slowly dissipated, disappearing into an aura of gentle peace that seemed to flow from the woman behind the desk. The hatred that clouded Skye's mind slowly dispersed like a morning fog, and like a breath of fresh air, her common sense recaptured her stubborn will.

Stupid! Skye thought. *I am an expert at being stupid!* Again, she glanced at Mrs. Chambers, this time connecting with the blue eyes that were staring back at her.

"Skye," Mrs. Chambers said as she leaned forward on the desk, "I love you very much."

Skye recoiled and lowered her head.

"The trouble is you always want to be the big shot," Mrs. Chambers scolded softly. "You need to let somebody else run your show, somebody like God. Give it up, honey."

Skye refused to respond.

"Isn't it about time for you to face all that bitterness eating away at you? You'll never change the facts about your mother, or your father, wherever they are. This might surprise you, but I was a foster kid, too. I never knew my parents either. I can't change my past, and you can't change yours. The only thing you can change is your heart. Skye, are you listening?"

Mother! Father! Why did she have to bring them up? Skye thought angrily. She slapped her hands over her ears, banging her elbows on her knees, and focused on a stain in the worn carpet.

"You can sit like that until the cows come home," Mrs. Chambers said. "But we're going nowhere until you face your problems. Stop running!"

I don't care if the cows ever come home. If she reaches for that Bible, I am outta here!

As Skye glanced up, Mrs. Chambers reached over near the phone to where Skye knew the Bible always rested.

Skye flew out of the chair. She spun, tumbling the chair backward with a loud thud, and bolted for the door.

"Where do you think you're going?" Mrs. Chambers said calmly.

"Somewhere you can't find me!" Skye screamed as she reached for the doorknob.

"Skye, stop running," Mrs. Chambers said softly.

Skye opened the door, rushed out of the office, and tore down the hallway toward the outside entrance. But just as she forced down the bar on the fire door, something stopped her.

I was a foster kid, too. The words reverberated through Skye's mind. *Eileen Chambers? A foster kid?*

Stop running, she heard in her heart. Skye turned to see if she could spot Mrs. Chambers. The hallway was empty. Skye stared at the door. *Stop running. I love you.*

Skye's eyes flooded with tears, and her face turned red hot. Slowly, she turned and walked back to the office.

Chapter Ten

Lope your horse!

"Right lead!

"Dismount!

"Mount!

"Figure eight!"

Morgan shouted orders to Skye, who maneuvered Champ in the center of the field. In only six weeks, Skye would have her first ride in the horse show at the county fair.

Skye finished a figure eight and then jogged Champ to where Morgan sat near the fence on Blaze.

"How'd I do?" Skye asked as she reined Champ to a halt. She patted him on the neck.

"Great," Morgan said. "It's so cool the way you've learned so quickly. I think Mrs. Chambers is right. You're a natural-born rider."

"When you sit on a horse that's trained like this one, riding is easy." Skye wiped her forehead with her arm.

"He's perfect! There's nothing he can't do. Some day we're going to tackle those jumps down there." She pointed to the lower field.

"Hold your horses, Skye!" Morgan said sharply. "You might think you're on wonder horse, but Champ's never been trained to jump. You could break your neck—or his. Stay away from those walls."

"Give me a break, Morgan," Skye said. "It's not that tough going over a little wall like those. He could do it. Did you ever try it?"

"There's more to jumping than meets the eye—balance, timing, and stuff like that. I'll never jump because I have no strength to launch myself forward over the horse's withers just at the right time to make a successful jump. You'd better think twice about it. If you want to learn, ask Mr. or Mrs. Chambers. They'd be glad to show you with Diamond or Ruby. But not Champ."

"On the other hand," Morgan said, changing the subject, "I think you're just about ready for that Western Pleasure Class. All you need are new boots and a big Stetson hat."

Skye laughed. "Can you see me in a cowboy hat?"

"You'll look great," Morgan said, laughing. "Come on. Let's ride down to the pond where it's cooler."

The girls moseyed their horses under a gigantic weeping willow and positioned themselves in the breezy shade. Morgan leaned forward, resting one arm across the saddle as the other hand relaxed the reins on Blaze's neck. Skye slid off her horse, dropping both reins to the ground, and stroked Champ's soft dilating nose.

"Man, is it hot today or what?" Skye said.

"Yep." Morgan ran her fingers through Blaze's wavy black mane. "We've done enough riding. These hot June days can be hard on the horses. Look how they're sweating, and it's not even noon yet. They'll need a long cool down."

"Thanks for helping me," Skye said in a tone that stirred surprise on Morgan's face.

"You're really different the last few weeks," Morgan said. "I mean, what happened? You've been thrown out of school before, so I figured that didn't do it. What's going on? You don't seem so angry."

"Well, I never thought I'd say this, but Mrs. Chambers is pretty cool. Did you know she was a foster kid too?"

"Yeah. She told me when I first moved in," Morgan said.

"She tells me I'll never straighten out until I learn to control my temper. That's what gets me in trouble all the time—that and my stupid pride. Mrs. Chambers has been helping me deal with stuff."

"I'll tell you one thing, Skye. Mr. and Mrs. Chambers understand kids. I'm glad you've decided to listen."

"In some things. But I'm not interested in all that Bible junk they throw out. I guess it's okay for you, but I don't need it right now."

A fly buzzed around Blaze's ears, forcing her to side-step out of the shade. Morgan maneuvered her back next to Champ and shooed the fly away.

"I can't begin to tell you how much the Lord has helped me through all my problems," Morgan said. "He's there whenever I need him. Someday you'll realize—"

"Tell me more about the horse show," Skye interrupted. All the God talk made her uncomfortable. "How many kids are usually in my class?"

"Between five and ten. It depends. The weather has a lot to do with it. People are funny with their horses. If there's a heat wave or it's raining, I'd only look for a handful. But it really doesn't matter. As well as you're riding, they'll have a hard time beating you—as long as you keep your cool. Know what I mean?"

"Yeah. Got it."

"Hey," Morgan said with enthusiasm, "This Friday Youth for Truth is going to meet in our basement for its monthly activity. Do you want to come? All the kids are in high school, but you're still welcome."

"What's Youth for Truth?"

"It's kind of a teen club from church that meets for Bible study and group activities. I'd love it if you'd come. That way you could meet some of the really cool Madison High kids. What do you say?"

"No way!" Skye snapped. "Those kids don't want a lowly seventh grader crashing their party."

"These kids are different. Honest! Besides, this is your home, too, so you can invite some of your friends and do your own thing. What do you say?"

"I guess I could invite Robin and Sooze. Are you sure your friends won't mind?"

"I know they won't," Morgan said. "The more the merrier. Now don't forget, seven o'clock on Friday."

"You persuaded me," Skye said, smiling. "I'll call them as soon as we cool down the horses. Thanks."

"No problem—Sis," Morgan said, a victorious smile on her face.

"Hey," Skye said, changing gears again. "Let's ride back to Piney Hollow. That place is so-o-o cool. I love it there."

"Ah, better not. It's too close to lunch. Let's head back to the barn and cool down. That should get us to the chow trough right on time!"

Friday night the Chambers' playroom buzzed with a dozen teens, as contemporary Christian music blared in the background.

Mr. Chambers and Skye had shown Robin and Sooze around the barn, allowing them to personally meet each horse. The girls then entered the basement and had found their way to the kitchen counter where Mrs. Chambers served barbecue and chips. The girls grabbed a can of soda each and settled on chairs in a corner near the pool table. They stayed out of everybody's way, huddling like three lost sheep and eyeing every move the older teens made.

"Hi," Morgan said as she motored toward the corner. Another girl walked behind her. "Skye, you know Melissa Richards from Maranatha?"

"Yeah." Skye's eyebrows raised. "Hi."

Morgan continued. "Melissa just joined Youth for Truth. I think you'll see her in teen class on Sundays, too."

"Hi," Melissa said, her pretty smile beaming in the light cast by the hanging pool table lamp.

"And who are these guys?" Morgan asked as she pointed to Skye's friends.

"Robin Ward," Skye said gesturing to her right and then to her left. "And Sue Bodmer."

"Hello," Robin said.

"Call me 'Sooze,' okay?" Sue said. "I hate the name Sue."

"Nice to meet you," Morgan said. "I hope you have a great time."

"Bye," added Melissa as she headed toward the busy Ping-Pong table. "See you later."

"See ya," Skye said.

Morgan pivoted her wheelchair to follow Melissa. "Talk to you later. Okay?"

"Later," Skye and Robin answered.

Sooze just took a giant gulp of soda.

"Hey, Skye," Sooze whispered as her eyes shifted to two boys at the pool table, "who are those guys?"

"Beats me," Skye whispered back. "Morgan told me their names but—wait, I remember. The cute one with the blond hair is Chad Dressler."

"He's way cute," Sooze snickered. "What grade's he in?"

Skye stared at Chad as he took a shot and laughed when he miscued. "I think he's a freshman, but I'm not sure."

Sooze sipped her soda and watched every move the boys made. "Hey!" she whispered. "He's looking over this way."

Skye had just taken a bite of her barbecue sandwich when she glanced up. Her eyes connected with the brownest eyes she had ever seen on a boy—eyes surrounded with curly eyelashes radiating from a chipmunk smile. As he bent over the table, Chad's wavy hair fell over his forehead, highlighting a dimple on each rosy cheek. As his eyes met Skye's, he smiled before taking his next shot.

"Wow," Skye mumbled with her mouth full, "he is too cute!"

Her heart gave an odd little beat and took off like a racehorse headed for the finish line. Her face burned.

"Man, I wish I lived here." Sooze said.

Oblivious to her surroundings, Skye studied every move Chad made. She'd never felt like this around a boy. Her heart started to melt.

Chapter Eleven

"Now remember," Mrs. Chambers said as Skye stroked Champ's neck. "Don't push him too fast. His only weakness is taking his left lead. Just give him his head. You concentrate on your balance and posture. Okay?"

"Got it." Skye replied.

"And stay away from the pack so the judge can see you," Mr. Chambers added.

"Stay away from the pack," Skye repeated.

As she sat on Champ outside the show ring at the fair, Skye chewed on her bottom lip. She was dressed in a suede cowboy hat leveled on her head to her eyebrows. She also wore a checkered shirt with a leather-fringed vest, a blue necktie, cowhide gloves, chaps, and brand new leather-cut boots. Skye looked like the perfect match for her mount. Champ had on his polished bridle with blue brow band and a leather-cut saddle that highlighted his glistening coat and silky mane and tail.

Skye scanned the horse trailers parked around the outside of the ring, the grandstand packed with cheering fans, the announcer's stand that blared incessant noise, and the judges busy comparing notes and looking at clipboards. At the long end of the large oval corral, she watched the other entries in her class. They were huddled on the outside of the gate, tightening cinch straps on their saddles, adjusting stirrups, checking bits in their horses' mouths, and sliding their hat strings tighter to their chins.

Skye's heart pounded as she focused on the ring where in only a few minutes she would make her debut. She had to admit she was afraid, but not with the same fear that had chased her so many times in the past. That fear had come from doing wrong and not wanting to get caught.

This fear was different. It was a fear of failing at something good. A fear of disappointing someone who cared about her.

You've trained for this all summer, Skye Nicholson, she lectured herself. *Keep your cool and let Champ do his thing.*

Morgan had just finished an Advanced Trail Class and was smiling from ear to ear as she jogged Blaze toward Skye and Mr. and Mrs. Chambers. In her left hand, she waved a red second-place ribbon.

"Way to go!" Mr. Chambers said as Morgan pulled Blaze next to Champ. "Another one for your collection." He shook Morgan's hand and patted Blaze on the neck.

"Great job," Mrs. Chambers said. "Skye, as soon as they check the roster, they'll call for your class. Let me see if your number is fastened tightly." She ran her fingers along the large number 77 attached to the back of Skye's vest.

Mr. Chambers checked Champ's bit, the cinch, and the stirrup lengths. "Now remember, listen carefully to what the judge tells you to do. And don't forget your number. Seventy-seven! Sometimes when it's a close call with one or two, the judge will call your number to repeat a maneuver."

"Seventy-seven!" Skye reached up to her hat, adjusting it one more time squarely on her head.

"Hey, Skye!" Morgan said as she pivoted Blaze toward the ring. "Look over on the top row of the grandstand. All the kids from youth group are there."

"I see Robin and Sooze too," Mrs. Chambers said.

Skye looked at the top row where she saw a long line of familiar faces waving and hollering.

"Oh, no!" Skye moaned with a hint of surprise. "Chad's there too!"

"Chad?" Morgan teased. "What about Chad?"

Skye's racing heart started to race even faster. Her face flushed.

"Attention," the announcer blared. "All entries for the Intermediate Western Pleasure Class please enter the ring."

Mr. and Mrs. Chambers turned toward Skye. "Okay, that's your signal," Mr. Chambers said. "Let's have a quick prayer." He took hold of Champ's bridle.

Mrs. Chambers stepped to the front of the horse beside her husband. "Okay, Tom." The Chambers and Morgan bowed their heads. Skye stared at Champ's ears.

"Dear Lord," Mr. Chambers said, "Skye's done her best to learn how to ride. We pray now for her and Champ's safety. We commit this competition into your hands, and ask that you bless her efforts. May your perfect will be done. In Jesus' name we pray. Amen."

"Amen," Mrs. Chambers added. "We know you'll do your best!"

Smiling, she turned Champ toward the gate. This is what she had trained for all summer, and she wasn't going to mess up now.

She checked out the parade of horses waiting at the gate, some nervously prancing, some calmly waiting— Quarter Horse, pinto, Arabian, white, Thoroughbred, black, Morgan, bay. As she gently prodded Champ into line, Skye inspected the faces of the eight other contestants in fancy outfits. Half of them, obviously first timers, looked scared and panicky. The other half looked steady and ready, like they'd done this a thousand times before. All were kids Skye had never seen before, from who knows where, and all anxious to win. Except for one.

Wait—no! It couldn't be. Hannah Gilbert? Hannah Gilbert on a horse? Here? At this horse show?

Skye's face wrenched like she had just been slapped. As she approached the pack, Skye glared at Hannah dressed in a fancy cowgirl suit and sitting on a golden Palomino on the other side of the cluster.

"You have got to be kidding!" Skye whispered to Champ as she brought him to a halt. "She rides? She shows? I thought all those brag sessions were about beauty contests—not horse shows!"

Just as Hannah squared her Stetson, she glanced up and her eyes met Skye's. *Pow!* Skye's invisible fist hit Hannah square between her snooty eyes!

The look of surprise on Hannah's face was equal to Skye's. Her eyes exploded to the size of the silver medallions on her hat, and her face radiated fire that matched her red silk shirt. Then, like her face was melting, it slowly twisted into a nasty glare.

Skye found herself amused instead of angry. Strangely, Hannah Gilbert and all her snootiness now had a different meaning in Skye's life. Instead of someone to hate, Hannah was just another competitor—someone Skye could beat fairly in front of the whole world. Skye's face broke into a grin. She raised her hand and wiggled her fingers at Hannah in mock greeting.

Hannah responded by jerking her head in the air and forcing her attention to the center of the ring. She yanked the reins of her horse sharply, pushing him tightly into the front of the pack.

Skye sat at the rear of the group, calming her nerves, petting Champ, anticipating every move she would make.

"Attention, ladies and gentlemen," the loudspeaker echoed, "the Intermediate Western Pleasure Class is now entering the gate."

The gate swung outward, and horses and riders entered the ring, walking single-file along the perimeter.

Skye gulped and squeezed Champ with her legs. She straightened her back and smiled, concentrating on her horse's moves as they brought up the end of the line.

"Ladies and gentlemen, walk your horses."

Skye concentrated on what she had to do to win.

"Lope your horses."

Carefully, methodically, Skye followed the judge's instructions as she and Champ circled the ring. Out of the corner of her eye, Skye watched Hannah, whose well-trained horse knew just what to do.

Around the riders went, walking, jogging, reversing, stopping, backing up, dismounting and walking away, and mounting.

Skye glanced at her watch as she mounted a second time. Twenty minutes had passed, and she had ridden Champ to perfection.

"Good boy, Champ," she whispered as she reversed and jogged around the ring one more time before lining up with all the rest in the center of the ring.

"Ladies and gentlemen," the judge announced as he surveyed the pack and raised his arm toward the right. "I would like to see forty-three, fifty-two, and seventy-seven, please. The rest of you may step aside."

Seventy-seven! That's me! Skye gulped. *No way!*

"You three stand here," the judge said as he stood in front of Champ.

A boy on a black Morgan maneuvered next to Skye.

Skye prodded, and Champ squared up, standing without moving anything but his tail to swish some flies. Skye shifted her glance to her left and saw Hannah Gilbert move up next to her. She was smiling at the judge as though that were his payment for giving her a prize.

"I want each of you to ride a figure eight, then lope your horse down to me," he said, gesturing to where he would be standing. "Slide stop and back up."

Skye and the boy nodded their heads.

"Yes, sir," Hannah said.

"Forty-three, fifty-two, and then seventy-seven. " The judge walked toward the end of the ring.

Skye's stomach did somersaults. She watched the boy and Hannah perform and, as far as she could tell, finish without a hitch. *This is no time to worry about Hannah Gilbert*, Skye told herself as she nudged Champ into his jog. *Now remember. Easy on the left lead.*

Around Skye rode in her figure eight, shifting her weight, nudging her horse, neck reining at just the right time. Lope—right lead—careful—left lead—easy—just right! Jog—slide stop—back up. Perfect!

Skye smiled as she lined up with the other two in the center of the ring and watched the judge as he walked toward the booth. She glanced at the bleachers. Silently, the spectators waited. She glanced to her left where the Chambers stood at the fence, smiling. Morgan, sitting on Blaze, smiled and gave her a thumbs-up sign. Skye glanced to her right where the boy and Hannah sat patiently while their horses stomped away flies on their legs and swished their tails.

The judge returned to the ring carrying three ribbons: blue, red, and yellow.

"First place, number seventy-seven, Skye Nicholson and her mount, Champ!" the announcer blared as the judge handed Skye her blue ribbon.

An explosion of cheers and applause erupted from the grandstand.

"Second place, number forty-three, Hannah Gilbert and her mount, Prince Goldenrod."

Hannah's smile to the judge was half what it was before. This time there was a twist of spite.

"Third place, number fifty-two, William Woods and his mount, Snoopy."

"We did it!" Skye said to Champ as she patted his neck. "We did it!" Her eyes shifted to the grandstand as she felt her face flush with excitement. The youth group kids, including Chad, were going wild—jumping, cheering, and waving.

Skye's eyes darted to Mr. and Mrs. Chambers who were hugging each other and jumping up and down. Morgan had raised her hands above her head and was applauding. An "I told you so" grin beamed from her extremely proud face.

"Congratulations. Very nice. Especially you, young lady," the judge said to Skye as he tipped his hat and shook her hand. "Very nice, indeed."

Young lady? Skye asked herself. *Really?* For the first time in her life, Skye dared to hope.

Chapter Twelve

"Come and get it!" Mrs. Chambers yelled from the pavilion under the pines as she flipped hamburgers on a grill.

"Be right there, hon!" Mr. Chambers yelled. "Okay, kids," he said as he dismounted, "we'll tie the horses at the barn while we chow down. After the victory celebration for these two"—he gestured to Skye and Morgan, who were still sitting on their mounts—"we'll let you guys try the saddles."

Still in their Western attire, Skye and Morgan had just finished demonstrating their show maneuvers from earlier that afternoon. Skye patted Champ on his neck and eyed Chad like he was made of gold as he laughed and told stupid jokes. He and the others petted the three horses, while congratulating the girls on their wins.

"If you don't come soon, the hamburgers will be dog food!" echoed from the pines.

Mr. Chambers handed the reins to Chad. "Skye, how about you and Chad taking the horses while I help Morgan off Blaze."

Skye's face flushed hot, and her heart took off again.

"Man," Chad said as he took the reins from Mr. Chambers and turned to Skye. "You and Champ are quite a team. How long have you been riding?"

"A few months," Skye answered. "Champ's great."

"Skye, why don't you get off and walk with Chad—let the horses cool down," Mr. Chambers said.

"Yeah," Chad said. "I've got a ton of questions."

Whether it was the blue ribbon hanging on Champ's bridle or Skye's racing heart, she couldn't tell. All she knew was that suddenly her head ballooned with pride, the kind that had controlled her life for so long. Suddenly, all she wanted to do was impress Chad one more time. Yanking Champ's reins to her left, she turned him on a dime. Sensing the excitement, the Quarter Horse pranced and snorted, ready to take off.

"I'll show you fancy riding!" Skye bragged.

Skye kicked her horse, and off they ran, charging across the field.

"What?" Chad stared, eyes wide and mouth open.

"Where's she going?" Mr. Chambers yelled.

Morgan turned Blaze sharply, staring at Skye and Champ as they raced across the field. "Oh, no!" she answered. "She mentioned jumping one day, and I told her to forget it. She's heading toward that wall!"

"What's she doing?" Chad yelled.

"I'll stop her!" Morgan shouted.

"No, you stay here!" Mr. Chambers said as he vaulted onto Chief and charged after Skye.

"Skye! Stop!" he yelled. "Champ can't jump! You'll kill yourself!"

"Come back here!" Morgan yelled.

Fiercely, Skye dug her heels into Champ's sides and prodded him toward the jump. She felt like she was flying. Her hat flew off her head. Her hair blew wildly, making her feel freer than she had ever felt before. "C'mon, Champ. Let's show 'em!" she yelled, her mind focused on one thing—the wall—as they charged toward it in a blazing gallop.

By now Sooze, Robin, and everyone else had become aware that something was happening.

"Where's she going?" Robin asked.

Mrs. Chambers had just placed a large tray of hamburgers on the picnic table when she heard her husband yell and looked up to see Skye racing across the field.

"Oh, no!" she shrieked, ripping off her chef's hat and running toward the impending disaster.

Mr. Chambers rode Chief at full gallop, chasing after Skye. "Come back here!" he yelled at the top of his lungs, "Skye, stop!"

The thrill of the moment, a mega-chance to show off, blocked Skye's thoughts from everything but her latest scheme. Her wild eyes studied the wall as she charged forward, determined to take Champ over it no matter how high or how dangerous it might be.

As Mr. Chambers gained ground and closed in, one of Chief's hooves caught on a clump of obstinate crabgrass and, like tumbleweed in the wind, both horse and rider fell forward. With a thud, Chief barreled head first onto the ground and pinned Mr. Chambers beneath him. In a few seconds it was all over, and Chief stood up badly shaken. Mr. Chambers did not.

Just as Skye glanced back to see if Chad was watching, she saw Mr. Chambers in hot pursuit and then watched as horse and rider tumbled to the ground.

"No!" Skye yelled. She slid Champ to a stop, only yards from the jump. "Mr. Chambers!" She turned and tore back to where Chief stood quivering, puffing like an engine, his nostrils dilating madly, and sweat oozing from his body. Beside him lay Mr. Chambers sprawled on the ground with his head bleeding, his face pale, his body motionless.

That same horrible fear that had chased her so many times in the past was hot on her heels again. The fear that had come from doing wrong and not wanting to get caught. The fear that made her run and hide. The fear that made her cry. The fear that clutched her soul so tightly, she could hardly breathe.

Skye wanted to help, to see if Mr. Chambers was okay. But she couldn't move. Skye studied the lifeless form. She wanted desperately for him to move—to breathe.

"Chad," Mrs. Chambers screamed as she ran toward the scene, "call 911! There's a phone in the barn office! Hurry!"

Skye sat frozen in the saddle. She steadied Champ as he puffed madly, still prancing, anxious to complete his course, to run like the wind.

Skye watched numbly as Morgan and Blaze galloped toward the unconscious man, while Mrs. Chambers and the others ran behind, their faces alive with fear. Skye felt like her brain was coated with fuzz. Panic clutched her heart, and all she could think to do was run away.

She yanked Champ's reins to the right and dug her heels into his sides. In a flash, the two were off, racing across the back of the field, past the wall, past every other jump, and down behind the pond. *As fast as Champ is, they'll never catch me!* Skye reassured herself.

"I'll get her!" Skye heard Morgan yelling.

"No, I need you here. Let her go!" Mrs. Chambers screamed.

I've killed him! Skye thought frantically. *I've gotta get outta here!* She jerked Champ to a stop at a gate. In her haste, Skye practically fell off the horse, fumbled with the latch on the gate, and swung it open, before scrambling back on Champ and kicking him sharply. "Let's go!" Skye yelled.

They galloped down the road, dust flying, until they disappeared into the shadows of the thick woods, running like the wind ... running away again.

Skye never looked back.

Chapter Thirteen

kye sat alone and miserable on a bench at the altar at Piney Hollow. In minutes Champ's lightning speed had brought her to the hideaway, far from the horror of what had just happened. She had cooled him down and now sat in front of the stone cross, wondering what had gone so terribly wrong.

Even though the setting sun ushered a cool evening breeze through the hollow, Skye sat in a nervous sweat, thinking about the events of the last several months, worrying about what might happen next.

"Why do I always mess up?" she cried out to the cross. "Why do I always have to be the big shot? I deserve to go to jail!"

The Chambers had been wonderful to her. They were tough but fair, and they cared. They had proven it time and time again.

Morgan cared, too, and treated her like the sister she never had.

Then there was Champ.

Skye turned and looked at the beautiful horse standing in all of his show-gear glory, resting at the rail with his one rear leg cocked at ease. He had given her a reason to live, a reason to care, a reason to love.

But what about Mr. C.? What if he were really dead?

Skye turned back to the altar, and her eyes focused on the cross, the symbol of God's love that meant absolutely nothing to her. This God, whom she didn't even know existed, loved her? As rotten as she was?

Skye stumbled to the altar and knelt at the cross, sobbing out her pain and despair.

"Please, God! He can't be dead!" she screamed. "He can't be!"

Behind her, she heard the creaking of a saddle as someone dismounted. Footsteps crunched on the gravel.

"Skye." A gentle hand touched her shoulder. Finally, Skye turned and looked up into swollen, red eyes.

"Mrs. Chambers, I'm so sorry!" Skye cried.

"I know, Skye," Mrs. Chambers said. She pulled Skye into her embrace and gently kissed the tears on her face. "It'll be all right. I love you."

Mrs. Chambers' arms wrapped firmly around Skye's quivering frame. And for the first time in her life, Skye didn't resist. With an open heart, she welcomed what this woman offered—the tender touch of a mother. Skye sobbed like a love-starved baby. They stood hugging one another for a long time as Skye cried in sorrow for all she had done and suffered through the years.

Finally, Mrs. Chambers said, "We have to go."

"What about Mr. Chambers?" Skye cried. "Is he dead?"

"No. I'll tell you on the way to the hospital."

Skye sat next to Mrs. Chambers in a waiting room on the third floor of Broadview General Hospital, her eyes red and puffy. Pastor Newman and Morgan completed the circle that filled a corner of the quiet room draped in midnight shadows.

Mrs. Chambers studied her watch. "It's been four hours."

"He has a severe concussion and head trauma," Pastor Newman said. "It takes a while for them to go in and relieve the pressure. Don't worry, Eileen. He's strong. He'll come out of this just fine."

Dog tired, Skye focused on the three people around her, noticing each one's anxiety blanketed in an aura of peace. She studied each face intently through her tears, wondering what made them so strong.

Their faith? Skye asked herself. *Maybe it isn't a bunch of baloney after all. Maybe God is real.*

Pastor Newman pulled out a small Bible from his shirt pocket. "This is the perfect time to look to God for help," he said as he turned the pages. "There are wonderful promises in God's Word to help us through times of crisis. Listen to this from the book of Isaiah, chapter 26:

'You will keep in perfect peace him whose mind is steadfast, because he trusts in you. Trust in the LORD forever, for the LORD, the LORD, is the Rock eternal.'"

Skye's eyes shifted to the floor, her face reflecting questions and doubt. *But if you're so great, God, how could you let this happen?*

"I love that verse," Mrs. Chambers said. "I don't know where we'd be without the Lord's strength." She reached over and gently squeezed Skye's hand.

Mrs. Chambers' warm, supportive hand wrapped securely around Skye's, drawing their hearts together. Skye looked at her foster mother's face, which somehow still bore a smile that lit up the room. Skye smiled back through her tears.

"God is in control," Mrs. Chambers said, "and he'll bring good out of this." She squeezed Skye's hand.

Pastor Newman put the Bible down and extended his hands. "Let's pray for Tom again. I know God has heard us, but let's thank him for what he's doing in that operating room."

Morgan and Mrs. Chambers joined hands with Pastor Newman. Mrs. Chambers squeezed Skye's hand tightly at the same time Morgan reached for the other.

Skye glanced up just as the others bowed their heads, and she too bowed hers.

"Dear Heavenly Father," Pastor Newman started.

For the first time in her life, Skye needed—wanted—to pray, but she didn't know how. Pastor Newman was so good at it. Would the Lord hear her?

God, Skye prayed silently, *if you're really there, I hope you're listening. Please, please help Mr. C. It was all my fault. Don't let him die or be paralyzed or anything. Please!* Warm tears ran down her face and dropped on her lap.

"We commit Tom into your hands. In Jesus' name. Amen," Pastor Newman concluded.

"Mrs. Chambers?" a doctor said as he entered the room.

Everyone turned toward the man in light green scrubs. His face bore tired relief.

"Yes?" Mrs. Chambers said as she stood.

"Your husband is going to be fine!"

"Thank God," she said. "Can I see him?"

The doctor slowly pulled off his scrub cap. "Not until he's out of recovery. The best thing for all of you is to get some rest. He's stable now. If there's any change in his condition, we'll call you right away. I'll look in on him early tomorrow morning." He turned to leave.

"Thank you, Doctor," Mrs. Chambers said. She smiled at the group. "God does answer prayer."

"I deserve to be in that bed, not Mr. Chambers," Skye cried as she buried her face in her hands and wept. "It's all my fault, and I don't blame you if you send me away. I'm so sorry. Please forgive me." Her words were muffled through her hands.

"Skye, honey, I've already forgiven you," Mrs. Chambers said. She pulled Skye into a warm embrace. "You don't have to keep asking. I love you, and it's settled."

"And she's not going anywhere. Is she, Mrs. C.?" Morgan added, smiling through her tears.

"Not now. Not ever," Mrs. Chambers replied. She held Skye at arm's length and gently brushed the tears from her face. "She can stay with us as long as she wants."

Through a flood of tears, Skye looked into Mrs. Chambers' own tear-filled eyes, eyes that would be special to Skye from that day forward.

Skye's search for the love she so desperately sought was over. Now she looked into the eyes of a mother who cared, a mother who loved her beyond her faults and all of her silly mistakes.

"Skye," Pastor Newman said as he stood, "that's the way God's love is, too. He loves us unconditionally and forgives us no matter what we've done. All we need to do is ask for his forgiveness with a humble and sincere heart."

At last Skye understood. She understood the unconditional love of a mother who really cared, and she was beginning to understand the unconditional love of a God who cares as well. She knew she would never be the same.

"Let's go home," Morgan said.

"Yes, let's go home," Mrs. Chambers agreed. She slipped her arm around Skye's shoulders and turned toward the door.

"Home?" Skye asked as a smile covered her tear-stained face. "Home."

Glossary of Gaits

Gait–A gait is the manner of movement, the way a horse goes.

There are four natural or major gaits most horses use: walk, trot, canter, and gallop.

Walk–In the walk, the slowest gait, hooves strike the ground in a four-beat order: right hind hoof, right fore hoof, left hind hoof, left fore hoof.

Trot–In the trot, hooves strike the ground in diagonals in a one-two beat: right hind and left forefeet together, left hind and right forefeet together.

Canter–The canter is a three-beat gait containing an instant during which all four hooves are off the ground. The foreleg that lands last is called the "lead" leg and seems to point in the direction of the canter.

Gallop–The gallop is the fastest gait. If fast enough, it's a four-beat gait, with each hoof landing separately: right hind hoof, left hind hoof just before right fore hoof, left fore hoof.

Other gaits come naturally to certain breeds or are developed through careful breeding.

Running walk–This smooth gait comes naturally to the Tennessee Walking Horse. The horse glides between a walk and a trot.

Pace–A two-beat gait, similar to a trot. But instead of legs pairing in diagonals as in the trot, fore and hind legs on one side move together, giving a swaying action.

Slow gait–Four beats, but with swaying from side to side and a prancing effect. The slow gait is one of the gaits used by Five-Gaited Saddle Horses. Some call this pace the stepping pace or amble.

Amble–A slow, easy gait, much like the pace.

Rack–One of the five gaits of the Five-Gaited American Saddle Horse, it's a fancy, fast walk. This four-beat gait is faster than the trot and is very hard on the horse.

Jog–A jog is a slow trot, sometimes called a *dogtrot*.

Lope–A slow, easygoing canter, usually referring to a Western gait on a horse ridden with loose reins.

Fox trot–An easy gait of short steps in which the horse basically walks in front and trots behind. It's a smooth gait, great for long-distance riding and characteristic of the Missouri Fox Trotter.

Parts of a Horse

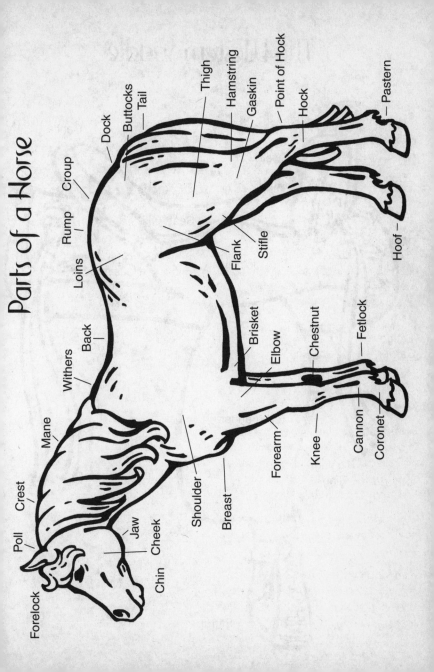

The Western Saddle

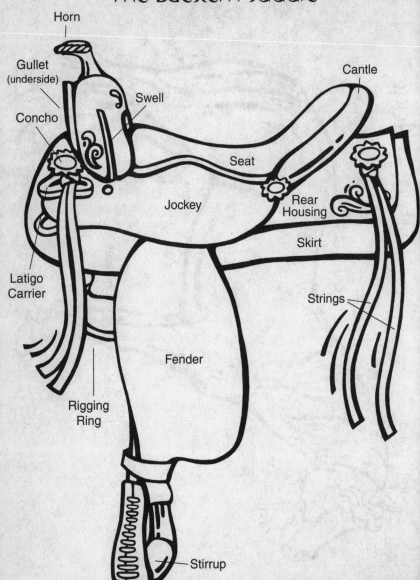

Horn

Gullet
(underside)

Concho

Swell

Cantle

Seat

Jockey

Rear
Housing

Skirt

Latigo
Carrier

Strings

Fender

Rigging
Ring

Stirrup

Book 2
Keystone Stables
A True Test for Skye
by Marsha Hubler
Zonderkidz

Chapter One

"Sooze, what do you think you're doing?" Skye Nicholson's voice rang out high and shrill. She leaned out Sooze's bedroom window, reaching toward her best friend who had staked herself out on the scorching-hot porch roof, a gallon can of kerosene in one hand and a cigarette lighter in the other. "Your mother called us. She said you were—"

"Get lost!" Sooze screamed. "I hate this dump! I hate the old lady! I hate everything! Who cares if I go up in smoke? Just get out of here—and leave me alone. I mean it, or this place goes up in flames!" Sooze flicked the lighter directly under the can.

Skye's attention darted to Eileen Chambers, Skye's foster mother, standing in the front yard, staring up at them. "Sooze, please come down. Your mother is going to call the police if you don't," she said, her voice filled with concern.

Skye pulled herself back into the bedroom and hurried her sweating hands through her long, silky dark hair. Her brown eyes glanced around Sooze's ransacked room. *What will get her in from that roof?* Skye focused on a picture hanging lopsided on the wall, and then she took a deep breath. *Maybe, just maybe!*

Skye leaned out toward Sooze. "Hey, put that stupid lighter down, would ya? What do ya think that's going to accomplish anyway—besides getting you in even more trouble?"

"You think I care? What have I got to lose?"

"Maybe more than you think, Sooze. I was just going to talk to you about this great idea I had. You like horses, right?"

ISBN 0-310-70573-8

Available now at your local bookstore!

Zonder**kidz**

Keystone Stables

Book 4

Teamwork at
Camp Tioga

by
Marsha
Hubler

Zonderkidz

Teamwork at Camp Tioga
(Book 4)
Written by Marsha Hubler
Softcover 0-310-70575-4

Coming
Spring 2005

Coming soon to your local bookstore!

Zonderkidz

We want to hear from you. Please send your comments about this book to us in care of zreview@zondervan.com. Thank you.

Zonder**kidz**®

Grand Rapids, MI 49530
www.zonderkidz.com